Death Over Easy

RECIPE FOR DEATH - BOOK 3

TAWDRA KANDLE

Death Over Easy

Cover Design: Meg Murrey
Formatting: Champagne Formats

ISBN: 9781682307588

Dedication

To all my Indie BookFest 2016 authors and readers . . .

Thank you for rolling with it this year in the face of Hurricane Matthew.

You rock. I hope you all come back next year so we can do it again, even better.

Grab a cup of coffee and a diner breakfast. It's time to return to Palm Dunes.

An epic showdown with a tremendous force of evil is looming on the horizon. Jackie and Lucas, along with their small band of friends and fellow Carruthers Institute agents, are on edge as they all await the opening blows in this battle to keep the dreaded Hive from making their terrifying plans for world domination a reality.

But meanwhile, life goes on in Golden Rays, the Florida retirement community within Palm Dunes, Florida where Jackie and Lucas are the youngest honorary residents. Jackie, who's still getting used to her new life as both a restaurant-owner and secret agent, is also now dealing with a prickly young sous-chef who needs her guidance and help. Lucas is confronted with a series of mysterious deaths with no apparent motive. Even his role of Death Broker can't help him find the killer.

And their friend and neighbor Mrs. Mac, busy competing in the Ms. Florida Senior Living pageant, just may be the next victim.

End of the world? Who has time?

Chapter 1

"THERE'S ANOTHER ONE, over on Crepe Myrtle Street."

Mrs. Mac made this announcement as she stomped into my kitchen, letting the door slam behind her. I glanced up from the thick volume I was reading, frowning at my next door neighbor and friend.

"Another one what?"

She tossed up one hand, as if exasperated by my clueless-ness. "Another house for sale. Another resident put her house on the market. Geez, Jackie, pay attention."

I wanted to say that when she walked into my house and started that conversation somewhere in the middle instead of at the logical beginning, it was kind of hard to follow along. But I didn't. Mrs. Mac had her quirks and faults, for sure, but she was a good and loyal friend. I wouldn't hurt her for the world.

"Okay. So another house has a for sale sign. What's the problem?"

She leaned down until she was peering into my face. She didn't have to lean that far, even considering that I was sitting down and she was standing. She'd lost quite a bit of height in her old age, and she'd never been a tall woman to begin with.

"That's the sixth one this *week*. Six! In one week. I'm telling you, something fishy's going on."

If something fishy were going on every time Mrs. Mac proclaimed it, we'd be living in the middle of seafood paradise. She tended to see conspiracy under every bush, and with her ear to the ground for gossip as it was—and believe you me, secrets and innuendo flew fast and furious in this kind of community and were the commodity of trade—she usually didn't have far to look.

"Uh, Mrs. Mac, I hate to point out the obvious, but we live in an over-55 community. Most of the residents remember Eisenhower's inauguration. It's not so unusual that there would be a pretty brisk turnover of houses since people are either relocating to have more help as they get old—well, *older*—or they're . . ." I wrinkled my nose, giving her my best regret face, hoping she didn't make me say the words. *How could I put this delicately?*

"Square dancing with Saint Peter?" She hauled out a chair from under the kitchen table and plopped down into it.

Okay, maybe that was as delicate as it got. "Sure. That works." I reached across to pat her hand. "So was it someone you know? I mean, whose house is up for sale?"

"No, he hasn't gotten to this part of the neighborhood yet." Mrs. Mac leaned her chin into her hand, staring down morosely.

"He? Who's 'he'?" I nudged the book away a little, hoping she was too distracted to ask me what I was reading. It wasn't anything I cared to explain to my elderly neighbor.

"That real estate guy. The one who's selling all the houses." She spoke as though she'd told me this a million times, and I just hadn't been paying attention. Maybe I hadn't been.

"Who is it?" I was vaguely familiar with most of the real estate offices in the area. I couldn't think of any sign I'd seen more than others lately.

"New guy. His name is Augustus Row, and his stupid picture is all over the for sale signs." Mrs. Mac sighed heavily. "By the way, I'm finally going to be a beauty queen."

I'd thought I was used to my friend's abrupt changes of subject and non-sequiturs, but this one struck me mute for a minute. I waited to see if she was going to clarify, but she didn't, and I felt obligated to respond in some way.

"Uh . . . what?" In the back of my mind, I was wondering if it was time to gently suggest she needed a check-up. *What were the signs for dementia, again?*

"Beauty queen. They're insisting. No matter how many times I've told them no, the committee refuses to accept it, so I finally said what the hell and gave in." She shrugged. "You know, the Ms. Florida Senior Living Pageant is huge now. Tickets are going to sell fast. You better get one for you and one for your love muffin as soon as they go on sale."

I was still trying to wrap my mind around this concept. "You're going to be in a beauty pageant."

She nodded. "I know what you're thinking."

Oh, I doubt that. I bit my lip to keep from speaking out loud.

"You're thinking that surely this isn't going to be my first pageant."

I smiled weakly. "You got me. Exactly what I was going to say."

"I know. Hard to believe, but my pop was completely anti-pageant when I was younger, and I just couldn't find it in my heart to go against his wishes. You understand."

"Sure," I agreed.

"But with my talent, you better believe they were knocking down the door."

"Your talent?" I tried to think what that might be. Mrs. Mac was a fair bridge player. She was a loyal friend, and of course she was a brilliant conversationalist, as was clear from our current exchange. But she didn't play any instruments, I didn't think she could dance, and—

"Of course. My singing." She smiled serenely. "I don't make a big deal of it, because it's not very nice to boast."

"No, you're right." Although what Mrs. Mac had to boast about in the singing department was lost on me. I'd heard her in the garden sometimes, and let's just say that whenever she hit a high note, my pup Makani lifted his nose and howled. I didn't think he was trying to make it a duet. "When is the pageant, exactly?"

"Two weeks. They don't like to let these things drag on, in case any of the contestants ups and dies. Once the poster is printed, you are committed, come hell or high water."

I briefly considered asking Mrs. Mac what happened if one of the would-be Ms. Florida Senior Living Queens had the audacity to kick off after the poster was printed, but then I thought better of it.

"Well, I can't wait to see you compete, Mrs. Mac. You

know you'll have my vote. And Lucas will vote for you, too."

Her brow wrinkled . . . more, if that was possible. "*You* don't vote, Jackie. This isn't *America's Got Idle Voices* or anything, you know. They've got judges, and they're the ones who decide. They choose the winner."

"Oh. Okay." I patted her arm. "Even so, we'll be there for you, cheering you on."

"I should hope so. After all, you're the closest thing I have to family, you know." She frowned, glancing around the kitchen. "Where's Lucas, anyway? Isn't he usually here this time of day, scarfing up whatever breakfast you've made?"

Ignoring the undercurrent of resentment I detected in her voice—whether she was more jealous of my time, my attention or my food, I couldn't be sure—I shook my head. "He's at his house writing today. He had an early breakfast." I closed the book and pushed it off to the side of the table, careful to keep the spine facing me, not Mrs. Mac. The title had the potential to provoke a whole new topic of discussion I wasn't ready to tackle this morning.

"Are you going into the diner?" She crossed her arms, leaning heavily on them. "Because I could eat, if you were. Plus, I'm thinking I need to make sure my constituency sees me out and about. It's important that they know I'm one of them, you know?"

"Mrs. Mac, dear, I'm pretty sure *constituency* only refers to elected, political positions, you know? Like senators or congressman, or the President."

"I told you, I'm going to be elected by judges." She quirked a brow at me. "Didn't we have a president who came to office that way?"

"No comment." Florida, in addition to being what Lucas

sometimes referred to as God's waiting room, was also a hotbed of political divisiveness. It had a good bit of old-fashioned Southern conservatism from those born and raised here, mixed in with some of the New York liberalism from the transplants. I never mentioned politics, because it was too dangerous to walk that path, not knowing where the landmines might be. "But you can ride into the diner with me, if you like. I'm meeting with Mary and then I'm coming right home. I have a lot of work this afternoon."

"What kind of work?" She eyed me suspiciously. "You own a diner, and you're not even there that much. How can you be working at the diner from home?"

"I don't own the diner. I run the diner." It was a fine difference. Yes, I hoped that one day the diner would be mine in reality, but I was still paying off the loan to the previous owner's family. Until that was finished, I refused to claim real ownership. "If you remember, I also write cookbooks. And . . ." I paused, wondering if I should divulge this last bit of information. "I've decided to expand into catering, so I'm setting up menus and updating the website and so on. I'm also including my tea blends there, so those can become part of what I offer. All of this is stuff I have to do at home, if that's okay with you."

"Sure." She shrugged. "Better enjoy your home now before Augustus comes and chases you out."

I'd nearly forgotten about the beginning of our conversation, since it had taken so many twists and turns since then. "I hardly think he's going to chase me out. I own this house. And I have no interest in selling to anyone."

"That's what they all say in the beginning, but then he manages to sweet-talk them. At least, that's what I hear."

"Who's buying the houses this dude lists?" I'd learned

over the years that while Mrs. Mac had her fair share of paranoid alarmism, she was actually right more often than not. "I don't get what his angle is, unless the properties sell. He's not buying them himself if the for sale signs are going up."

"*He's* not, but someone is." She gave one quick, sage nod. "I don't know who, and I can't get a clear answer on that. All he does is put them up on the market. Talks the owners into selling. But." She held up a finger and gave me wide, earnest eyes. "But I will say that I've never seen anyone move into the houses that have supposedly been sold. They're not turning over. Something else is going on. Something evil."

A chill ran down my spine, and I wanted to laugh or cry. I wasn't sure which. Mrs. Mac was closer to the truth than she could have guessed; something evil *was* going on, but it didn't have anything to do with ambitious real estate agents or whoever was buying those houses. No, the evil I was investigating was ancient and cunning, able to shimmy and shift away from us just when we thought we'd gotten a handle on exactly what was happening.

"Don't you think you might be exaggerating just a little?" I put on a bright tone, trying not to think about what was happening with my friends up at Carruthers Initiative Institute, the front lines for this fast-approaching battle. "I'm not saying you're wrong—it *is* a little odd. But it could be coincidence. Maybe he's just a new real estate agent who's trying to make a name for himself. And honestly, I'm not sure what you want me to do about it."

"I think you and Lucas should look into it. You two do all that detective work now, and Lucas knows so much about death."

My heart skipped a beat. "Um, what? What're you talking

about, Mrs. Mac?" We were so careful not to raise any suspicions among our friends about my boyfriend's unusual extracurricular activities, but sometimes, I was afraid my neighbor suspected that there was more to him than met the eye.

"Oh, you know. All that fuss with Crissy Darwin's band when that psycho was killing them off. You were both right in the middle of it. And Lucas is writing a book about death, isn't he? Which sounds about right, since he seems to pop up whenever someone dies. Like an undertaker."

"Don't be ridiculous." I spoke a little sharper than I intended. "The thing with Crissy was just coincidence, and . . . why do you think he's writing a book about death?"

"He told me he was. That night I brought over the homemade wine from my nephew up in New York, remember? And I asked him if his book had any hanky-panky in it, because I like a book with a little bit of sexy time fun, you know? And he said it didn't. He said it was all about death. He told me that all his work was about death, which was a little weird, but then, some guys get all moody when they . . ." She made a drinking motion with one hand to her lips. "You know. Tipple."

I bit the side of my lip. "Yeah, I remember that night." That wasn't completely true; I remembered bits and pieces of that night. Mrs. Mac's nephew was an amateur winemaker, and what he'd sent his favorite aunt had been stronger than any of us had expected. It took a lot of alcohol to make Lucas even the tiniest bit tipsy; he thought it was something to do with his vampire nature, although it might have been connected to his role of death broker, too. Who knew which part of him was associated with what? We were still figuring out all of it.

But for whatever reason, that night Lucas had gotten drunk. At least, I thought he had; both Mrs. Mac and I had been more a little worse for drink as well, although apparently she had been sharp enough to remember what Lucas had said. All that stuck out to me was the massive hangover I'd had the following day.

"Well, yeah." I nodded. "It's a . . . murder mystery. I think. You know he doesn't let me see any of it. He's very private about this book. I guess we'll all just have to wait and see."

"There are ways, you know." Mrs. Mac waggled her eyebrows at me. "You could persuade him. Shut down shop, if you know what I mean. When men stop getting the nookie, they'll do just about anything to get it back. Trust me."

Why and how I was supposed to take relationship advice from a woman who'd only been married for six months before her young husband's death and who hadn't been any luckier in love over the six decades that followed that sad occurrence was beyond me. But sometimes with Mrs. Mac, the best response was a nod and smile. And changing the subject seemed like a very good idea, too.

"You know, come to think of it, maybe we should go over to the diner now, instead of waiting until this afternoon. Why don't you go grab your purse, and I'll—"

The kitchen door swung open, and we both turned just as Lucas stepped inside. His eyes darted to our neighbor and then back to me, widening just a little.

"Hey. Uh, sorry, am I interrupting something?" His jaw was tense, and his mouth clamped together.

"No." A sense of foreboding filled me. Lucas had been summoned—called to a death, where he had to send the dearly departed on to either paradise or the other place—earlier that morning. It wasn't unusual at all, and I hadn't been worried until now, when I'd seen his face. But given everything we were experiencing and learning about, expecting the worst didn't seem unreasonable anymore. "Do you need me?"

"I need to talk to you. If you have a minute." He smiled, but I knew it was forced. "I'm sorry, Mrs. Mac. Can I borrow Jackie for just a little while?"

My friend was usually a rational woman—well, maybe *usually* was being generous. Still, she never did anything to come between Lucas and me. But I could see that she wasn't at all happy about this suggestion. "We were just about to leave for the diner. Can't it wait? I'm starving."

"Just a few minutes." Lucas shot her the charming smile that turned most women to babbling piles of mush. "She'll be right back. I promise."

I stood up and patted Mrs. Mac's shoulder. "You go on home and get ready, and I'll be right over to collect you. It won't take a minute."

"You two aren't just trying to get me out of the way so you can do the horizontal hoochie-coochie, are you? Because if that's the case, I hope it'll take more than a minute."

I was positive my cheeks had gone bright red, which was ridiculous, because of course Mrs. Mac knew that Lucas and I slept together. Hell, our other neighbor down the block had caught us in the act—or just about—one night when we'd gotten frisky in the car, parked in Lucas's driveway. Still, it wasn't anything I wanted to discuss. I wasn't a prude, but neither was I interested in sharing all the down and dirty details.

"I promise you, that's not what we're going to do. Lucas just has a work question, right?"

He nodded. I turned back to Mrs. Mac and patted her shoulder. "I'll be right there."

"Hmph." Pushing herself to her feet, the old woman

shook her head. "Youth is wasted on the wrong people. If my equipment were in better order and I had an interested fellow, we'd be going at it like bunnies all the time."

". . . and that's what we call TMI, Mrs. Mac. Look, you're making Lucas blush." It was true, too. My boyfriend had a red face and a deer-in-the-headlights expression in his eyes. "I'll be there in a minute."

Mrs. Mac mumbled indignantly under her breath, but she did move, stomping her way across my kitchen floor, out the back door and down the stairs. I waited, watching through the window until I saw her nearing her own house before I heaved out a breath and turned to Lucas.

"What's wrong?"

He frowned. "Why do you think something's wrong?"

"Oh, I don't know." I tossed my hands into the air. "Let's see. We're dealing with a rampant evil force that wants to take over the world, and we're supposed to be figuring out what it is and how to stop it. Oh, and then there's Veronica, the crazy vampire lady who's been skulking around recently, just waiting for her chance."

"Her chance to do what, exactly? She already vamped me. Actually, I wish she'd come by for a visit, just so I can ask her what the hell she was thinking." Lucas ran his fingers through his hair, a sure sign that he was stressing. "I think about her a lot. I only want to know why she turned me that night."

I bit my lip and reined in my annoyance. "Let's not invite Veronica the vampire over just now, okay? The last thing I need to do is try to explain her to Mrs. Mac."

"It's not like I could find her anyway." He shook his head. "She's not who I need to talk to you about. This doesn't have anything to do with—" He glanced to the window, as though there might be listening ears, and lowered his voice. "Carruthers stuff. It's something else. Something that happened at the death I was summoned to this morning."

"All right." *Color me confused and wary.* The only times Lucas shared details about his death brokering was when it concerned someone we knew. Since we lived in a senior citizen community in Florida, it wasn't a stretch to expect that many of my friends would be moving on to the happy hunting grounds sooner rather than later, but still . . .

"I see that face." Lucas took a step toward me and pulled me close. "Don't worry, the departed wasn't anyone either of us knows. Or knew. He was an old guy from Citrus Point, and he died of a massive heart attack—nothing unusual or suspicious about it."

"You're sure?" I burrowed my face in the crook of his neck. "Positive?"

"Absolutely. He had a history of heart disease. And he'd just finished a plate of cheese fries. I'm telling you, this dude went out happy."

"Cheese fries? I thought he died this morning."

"He did. But apparently that was his breakfast of choice." Lucas shrugged.

I crinkled my brow. "He told you this?" Usually, his conversation with the dead was limited or non-existent. I'd never heard of him shooting the breeze with the souls about to shuffle off.

"No . . . but that's kind of what I need to talk to you about." He drew back from me a little, running the tip of his tongue over his lips as he squinted out the window, carefully *not* looking at me. "The guy who died—his name was Reg—he had someone with him. His niece, Charlie. And she didn't have anywhere else to go, and she seemed so lost . . ." A tiny bit of guilt infused his eyes, something akin to how I'd seen my nephews look when they were admitting to something they'd hoped to avoid. "I brought her home with me."

"Uh huh." I nodded slowly. This wasn't the first time Lucas had carried home his work, both literally and figuratively. We'd met our friend Crissy Darwin, the up-and-coming folk singer, when her manager had been murdered earlier this fall. I wasn't surprised now, but I was a little mystified about why it seemed to be such a big deal. "Was she actually there when he died? Just how did you explain being at the bar when it happened?" The death broker gig apparently came with an unlimited get-out-of-jail-free card that meant Lucas was never considered a suspect in any kind of death, and no one seemed to question how often he turned up when someone had just died. Usually he avoided being seen by the family or anyone else, but sometimes, it was inevitable.

He grimaced. "It was one of those weird coincidences. She was with her uncle when he went down, and she screamed. I was already in the room, but she hadn't seen me, so I just said I'd been passing by when I heard her. I told her I'd do CPR and sent her to call the ambulance, but he was gone before he'd hit the floor. The advocates and I did our thing fast, and then I stayed around until the paramedics called it and the funeral home people came. But I couldn't bring myself to leave her alone there. Of course, we had to taxi home because I couldn't just transport back with her along for the ride." Something else passed through his eyes, but I couldn't tell exactly what it was.

"So where is she now?"

"At my house. For the time being." He rubbed his hands

over my upper arms. "But I was hoping maybe she could come stay with you for a little while."

I wrinkled my nose. "Me? Why me?"

Lucas smiled. "A couple of a reasons. First, she doesn't have any place else to go right now. She lived with her uncle above the bar that he owned, and I didn't think she should be alone there, when he just dropped dead on the first floor. Second, she graduated from culinary school a few weeks back, so you'd have something in common. Third, and probably most important, she's a twenty-one-year old girl, and I don't think anyone would be comfortable with her staying at my house."

"Twenty-one?" I'd been picturing a smart-ass, gum-popping kid, not a young woman. "Uh, yeah, I wouldn't be happy with you boarding her at your house."

"She's not a dog, Jackie." Lucas rolled his eyes. "No one is *boarding* her with me. But she's young and alone, and I thought maybe you could even use her at the diner. Or you might consider whether she could help with your new business. Another set of hands doing food prep wouldn't be a bad idea, especially considering you might be otherwise occupied. You know, with saving the world and all that."

I swallowed back a groan of exasperation. It was just like Lucas to turn that back around on me, and dammit, he had a point. He'd encouraged me when I'd come up with the idea of using the diner as a springboard for something I'd wanted to try—that was the catering—even though I knew we were both wondering if the world was going to be in any shape to need food preparation. If Mallory Jones and the Hive had their way . . . well, we didn't know precisely what their plans entailed, but it wasn't going to be pretty, and I doubted they were going to hire me to cater it.

"I guess she could stay here for a little bit. I have the extra room." My guest room was hardly ever occupied, unless my parents or one of my siblings visited. Distractedly, I wondered if I'd changed the sheets after the last time my friend Leesa had been down to stay with us.

"Awesome. Anyone ever tell you you're the best girlfriend ever?" Lucas tugged me a little closer.

"Sucking up will get you nowhere." I tried to sound stern, but my voice quivered a little. It didn't matter what I said; when it came to Lucas, my willpower was practically non-existent.

"Oh, really? I seem to remember that *sucking* got me plenty far this morning." He dipped his head, brushing his lips down to skim over the spot where my neck met my shoulder. "As a matter of fact, if I recall, you were basically promising me anything I might want. In a very loud voice."

"Stop." I pushed at him, but it was a half-hearted attempt, and he could tell. He wrapped his arms tighter around me, leaving no doubt about where his mind and attention were. "Don't start anything you can't finish, mister."

"Who says I can't finish?" His eyes narrowed as he gazed down at me, and I realized I'd just issued the type of challenge that no man ever turned down.

"I meant that you have a girl waiting over at your house, right? So now might not be the optimal time for us to, uh, start anything. Also, let's remember that Mrs. Mac expects me to drive her to the diner. I wouldn't put it past her to barge in."

Lucas groaned. "You're not wrong, but God, I wish you were. Okay. I'll run next door and bring Charlie over. You can get to know her, she can settle in, and then . . ." He touched his lips to my forehead. "Later. You and me. And I'll remind you just how well I can finish anything I start."

Without waiting for me to respond, he stalked across the kitchen and out the door. I sank into a chair, sighing and wondering what I'd just agreed to do.

It didn't seem that long ago that I'd been enjoying a quiet, boring life as a cookbook reviewer for an online food magazine. I'd lived here in the house I'd inherited from Nana after she'd passed; I'd had a few senior citizen buddies locally, my best friend Leesa back in the Big Apple to talk to long-distance, and my parents and brothers in upper New York state. My life had been predictable but more than a little flat and empty.

All that had changed when Lucas had moved in next door. Suddenly, I had a boyfriend, and more than that, I had a boyfriend who'd recently undergone a dramatic life-changing experience which had resulted in him now being both a death broker and a vampire. Or a half vampire, at least. Falling in love with him had led to our involvement in situations I'd never dreamed existed . . . including the horrible experience of having my body possessed by the soul of a woman who was part of the evil force trying to destroy the world. That had been a definite low point in the last few years.

But on the other hand, there weren't many ho-hum days anymore, not when I was in love with a guy who announced the fate of departed souls and also consumed blood by the bagful . . . or from me, when we were in the height of passion. I'd found the man of my dreams, and I was finally beginning to do the work I'd always imagined: running a diner, launching a catering business and writing cookbooks on the side. The fulfillment was sweet, and I wasn't going to complain about the regular sex, either.

Movement outside the house across the lawn caught my eye, and I watched as Lucas followed the girl toward my home. I would've pegged her as being younger than twenty-one; she was petite, with jet-black hair that was cropped short. Her jeans were loose and rolled at the ankle, and a huge black T-shirt fell to mid-thigh. She looked as though she'd been playing dress-up in her big sister's closet. She had a large army green duffel slung over her shoulder.

Sitting back in my chair, I waited for Lucas to open the door and lead her inside. He shot me a glance that was half-pleading and half-warning, and I smothered the urge to stick out my tongue at him. He acted as if I might actually be tough on this poor kid who'd just lost her only living relative. What did that say about his opinion of me?

He came to stand next to me as I rose to my feet. The girl stopped a few feet away, arms crossed over her chest and her mouth tight. The bag on her shoulder must've been heavy, but she didn't slouch or drop it. I caught the glint of a tiny eyebrow ring, nearly camouflaged by her blonde brows—clearly the black hair was dye job. She didn't look up at me; instead her eyes were steady on the floor just beyond my feet.

"Jackie, this is Charlie Caldwell. Charlie, my girlfriend, Jackie O'Brien. She has a room here, and you can stay as long as you need."

I stood up and held out a hand. "I'm glad to meet you, Charlie, although not under the circumstances. I'm sorry about your uncle."

"He wasn't really my uncle." There was no mistaking the hostility in her voice or the way she ignored by outstretched hand. "I called him that, but he was really my aunt's boyfriend."

"Oh." I sought Lucas' eyes, but he seemed as clueless as

me. "Well . . . where's your aunt?"

"She died three years back."

"I'm sorry." I repeated the words. "Your parents . . .?"

Charlie shrugged. "No clue. They took off, I guess, when I was a baby, and left me with Aunt Val. It was just the two of us for a while, and then she started hooking up with Reg when I was about ten. We moved in with him over the bar, and when she died, I stayed with him. Didn't have any place else to go."

If any other young girl had told me that story, I would've wrapped her in a hug filled with sympathy. But Charlie emitted a clear keep-away vibe, and I respected that. She didn't want me to feel sorry for her, and so I wouldn't.

"Well, like Lucas said, you're welcome to stay here as long as you need." I tried to sound as though I meant the words. "It's not fancy around here, but you'll have your own bedroom, a bathroom and full use of the kitchen. Lucas tells me you just graduated from culinary school. Do you have a job yet?"

She shook her head. "I only finished about two weeks ago. And the plan was that I would cook at Reg's place for the time being, until I saved up enough to do my own thing." The hard veneer cracked just a little, and I saw her lips twitch. "But I guess that's not an option anymore."

"Can't you take over his . . . did you say he owned a bar?" It seemed a little cold to be talking about the recently-deceased man's possessions so cavalierly, but I could see Charlie was worried, despite her attitude.

"I don't know. Probably not. The Stinker has a mortgage, I'm pretty sure, and even if he left it to me free and clear, I'd have no fucking clue about how to run a business. I'm a chef, not a manager, you know?"

I nodded. "Yeah, I get that. The Stinker? That's the name

of the bar?"

For the first time since she'd come into my house, her face relaxed slightly, and I thought absently that when she dropped her defenses, Charlie was actually pretty.

"The Hook, Line and Stinker. Uncle Reg's dad named it that, but everyone called it just the Stinker." She darted a glance at me. "I don't need anyone to take care of me. I'm not a kid or a charity case." She hunched her shoulders.

"No one thinks that." I spoke crisply, realizing that straight talk was what she wanted. "Lucas and I don't feel sorry for you. But you lost your—your Reg just hours ago. No one would think any less of you for grieving, Charlie. And we're just trying to give you a place to land until you see what comes next."

She nodded slowly. "Okay. I guess that's all right. But he—" Charlie pointed at Lucas. "He said you could maybe use some help, too. So put me to work. I don't expect a free ride." The jut of her lip said she wouldn't take anything she hadn't earned, either. That won her some grudging respect from me, even if that was going to make it harder to give her a hand.

"Of course. I own a diner—well, sort of—and I'm just starting to get a catering company off the ground. So an extra set of hands would be a godsend. Especially a set of hands that have been professionally trained."

"Cool." She didn't move, and I had a hunch that she wouldn't until I did.

"Let me show you the room, and maybe you want to rest a little. I'm going to run over to the diner in a few minutes, but Lucas will be right next door." I slid my eyes toward him and added, "Unless he gets called out for work, that is. But if you need anything, I'll leave you my cell phone number."

"I thought you said you were a writer?" Charlie frowned at Lucas suspiciously. Yeah, this kid didn't trust easily, that was for sure.

"I am." He spread his hands. "But I haven't published a book yet, so I have this kind of, um, side gig. Sometimes I have to leave on short notice."

"Right down this hall." I guided Charlie out of the kitchen before she could ask Lucas any more questions he'd have to struggle to answer.

Lucas squeezed my shoulder as I moved behind the girl. "I owe you big time," he whispered.

I smirked and slid away from him. "Don't think I'll forget it."

Chapter 2

"ARE THESE YOUR only knives?" Charlie frowned down at the blade in front of her as though I'd handed her plastic silverware.

"Well . . . yeah. Here, anyway. They have others at the diner, but I don't do any serious cooking here. All of the catering work is going to be done in the diner kitchen." I'd skirted a bunch of health and safety inspections by making Jackie O'Brien Catering an offshoot of Leone's, giving me a place to cook that was already approved by all the powers that be.

"Okay, but how in the hell do you do any cooking at all with . . . these?" Charlie waved her hand over the worn knife block on my counter. "They're dull, and what's more, they're kind of cheap."

"They belonged to my grandmother. They have sentimental value. I sharpen them as much as I can, and . . . they're fine." I tried not to huff. "If they're not good enough for you, you're welcome to bring over your own set."

Her eyebrows drew together, and she turned her back to me. I could've bitten off my tongue: all of her stuff was still at the bar, where her uncle—or whoever he was to her; she hadn't said much about him since she'd arrived two days before—had dropped dead in front of her. Yes, she was on the verge of annoying the living crap out of me, but still, I was being insensitive.

"Charlie." I laid a tentative hand on her arm. "I'm sorry. I didn't mean to snap at you. Do you want me to take you over to the bar today? You could pack some more clothes and pick up what you wanted from the kitchen."

She met my eyes, her expression inscrutable. "I don't have that much stuff. Everything there belonged to Uncle Reg."

"Well, sure, I understand that, but did he have kids? Or any other family? I mean, is there anyone who's going to want the bar and everything in it, besides you?"

Charlie shrugged. "Not that I know of. Reg never mentioned family. He was always good to Aunt Val and me, but we never had, like, deep talks about the past. Or the future."

"You're going to have to find out if he had a will. Who knows, he might've left you everything." I wasn't trying to get rid of Charlie, but over the past few days, she hadn't made any moves to do much of anything. She'd been hiding out in the guest room, rebuffing all my attempts to lure her out with food or offers of socializing. She'd even ignored Mrs. Mac, who was the past champion of cajoling intractable young women into being her friend.

Not that the older lady had taken offense. "She's just sad, honey, that's all." Mrs. Mac had shaken her head. "Imagine.

She's been abandoned and left behind so many times, and this just feels like one more kick in the stomach. Why on earth would she trust strangers like you or me when the people who're supposed to be there for her haven't been?"

She had a point, but still . . . having been raised by women who made sure I understood the niceties of life, manners and how I was supposed to behave made it tough for me to remember that Charlie hadn't had that advantage. I couldn't imagine staying in someone's house and not at least trying to be pleasant, even if I was hurting. That was why this morning, I'd finally resorted to using guilt to pull her out, saying I needed help with a new recipe I was trying for my catering venture. She'd followed me into the kitchen without hesitation, and we'd been working well, if silently, side-by-side, until her comment about the knives.

Now she squinted at me, as if considering my comment about the possibility of a will.

"Reg wasn't exactly the plan-ahead type. He probably wasn't a very good businessman. And I'm not related to him at all, so I doubt the courts or whatever would think of me as someone who should get his shit. I don't have any claim." She paused, her eyebrows knit together. "I do have a car over there, though. It's mine." This was as much information as she'd given me to date, and I perked up a little.

"Well, that's something. I could drive you over to pick it up, and then maybe you'd feel like you have a little more freedom here. You could explore, and just . . . you know. Get out and see what's what."

"I don't have to stay here." The defiance was back. "I can always find someplace else to crash."

I was walking a fine and shaky line here, and at the

moment, I'd have cheerfully wrung my boyfriend's neck for putting me in this position. Unfortunately, I couldn't do that, since he'd been missing in action for the past two days, checking in with me via text with vague if supportive messages, assuring me that he was fine, just busy with a lot of death brokerings (he called them Reckonings) and some research Cathryn, our de facto boss, had asked him to do on the save-the-world front.

"Charlie." I tried to sound compassionate and at the same time avoid patronizing her. "You are welcome here, for as long as you want to stay. I know this is a kind of unusual situation. I understand that you don't know me, you don't know Lucas, and living in the middle of a senior citizen community probably isn't your dream come true. I'm not forcing you to stay with me. But at the same time, I'm not kicking you out, either. Everything is up to you."

She studied me without answering for a few seconds, and then she gave a quick nod. "Okay." Picking up my clearly-unsatisfactory knife, she began dicing an onion.

I won the battle to keep from rolling my eyes, but barely. *Okay?* What was that supposed to mean? *Okay*, she understood? *Okay*, she was leaving? *Okay*, thank you for letting me, a complete and largely-hostile stranger, stay in your home for an unspecified amount of time?

I couldn't think of a nice way to ask any of those important questions, so I sighed and went back to the meat I'd just browned, which was draining over paper towels at the moment. I was working on a pocket taco idea, something that could be served easily at parties or picnics, which tended to make up most of the catering needs in this part of the world. I didn't plan on putting together menus that revolved around an intriguing little finger sandwich; that wasn't going to fly in this area of the world.

My phone buzzed in the pocket of my jeans, drawing my attention away from cooking as I saw the name on the caller ID readout. *Lucas.*

"About time, lover." Sarcasm oozed from my words. "I was beginning to think you'd skipped town."

"No." He sounded strained. "Are you alone, Jackie?"

"Ummmm . . ." I glanced over my shoulder at Charlie, who seemed to be wholly absorbed in her chopping. "Just a sec."

Dropping the hand that held the phone to my side, I addressed the younger woman. "Hey, I need to step out to take this. Can you add that onion to the meat and then return the whole thing to the skillet? I'll start working on the sauce next and add it when I'm done here."

She gave me a curt nod and a lift of her shoulder. I decided to accept that as the most enthusiastic response I was going to get and went out the back door to sit on the stoop.

"Okay, shoot. I'm here. What's going on?"

There was some kind of muffled noise on the other end, but I could still hear Lucas. "I had a Reckoning this morning. It was Mrs. Schmidt, Jackie. I wanted you to hear it from me."

I frowned. "Norma? But . . ." My voice trailed off. I didn't know Norma Schmidt tremendously well; she'd joined Mrs. Mac's neighborhood dinners now and then, and I remembered that she'd been a concert pianist once upon a time. She was from Austria, and she'd retained a trace of her accent, even though she'd lived in the States for well over forty years. "She was young. I mean, younger than most of the other people around here."

"I know. She didn't die of old age, Jackie, or of anything natural. She was murdered."

My eyes slid closed. "Shit. Really? Again?"

"Yeah, my sentiments exactly." Lucas blew out a sigh, and I could picture him raking one hand through his hair. "I was in and out before the cops got there, so I don't know any details, but there was still someone in the house when the advocates and I showed up. I didn't get a look at a face."

"How—" I cleared my throat. "How did it happen? Was she shot?"

"No. I'm pretty sure it was strangulation, judging by what I saw. Her eyes—"

"Stop." I held out a hand even though I knew Lucas couldn't see me. "I don't need that visual. Bad enough I have to know she was killed. God, this is crazy. Are you sure when you got vamped and turned into a death broker at the same time that they didn't also decide to give you an extra special gift of murder solving? You should totally ask the advocates if it's normal for death brokers to see so many violent deaths."

"Maybe." He hesitated. "There was kind of something else, Jacks."

Dread tiptoed up my spine. Lucas only used his nickname for me when he was hoping for sexy time or about to deliver bad news. Since a booty call seemed unlikely in this scenario, I had to assume it was the latter.

"What?"

"There was a poster next to the kitchen table. It was for the Ms. Florida Senior Living Pageant, and Mrs. Schmidt was a contestant. Her picture was right above Mrs. Mac's, and when I looked at it, I realized I'd been to another Reckoning last week for someone else in the pageant."

"Are you saying that you think someone's targeting the women in this thing? Why in the hell would anyone do that?" I considered the possibilities for a moment. "Unless it's someone trying to weed out the competition. And even then, murder seems a little extreme for a local senior citizen pageant, where the prize is a couple hundred bucks and a gift certificate for a year of perms from the Beauty Barn."

"Maybe it's just coincidence. But it doesn't feel like it."

"Could some old woman even manage to strangle someone? I can see poison or maybe pushing the competition down a flight of steps, but this would take a lot of strength in the hands, right? I can't see someone like Mrs. Mac, for example, being able to do that."

"Not with her hands, certainly, but with a scarf or a belt? Probably." Lucas paused. "Not that I think Mrs. Mac did this. But I do think she might be at risk, so I want you to keep your eye on her, okay? Just make sure nothing hinky is going on. No strangers in her house, and tell her to keep her doors locked."

"Okay." My stomach clenched. Mrs. Mac could be a royal pain at times, but I loved her like she was my own grandma, and I couldn't bear it if anything were to happen to her.

Something else occurred to me. "Lucas, you've heard Mrs. Mac's numbers. How long she has to live. I know you did, back when you first met her. Do those numbers match up to her dying now?"

One of the odd side effects of being a death broker was that Lucas could hear how much time each person he met had left on this earth. It hadn't happened with me—thank God—and he'd since learned to block that part of his gift, but when we'd gotten to know each other, he'd admitted to me that he had heard Mrs. Mac's time left.

"No," he answered me now. "As far as I can remember, they don't. The thing is, though, those numbers can change. You know that precogs tell us our choices affect the future, so it's tough to predict most things with accuracy. It's the same with my numbers. If something has shifted since I heard them, they might not be right. So just watch her. But don't tell Mrs. Mac anything. I don't want her to freak out and go crazy telling everyone that a murderer is stalking the contestants of the Ms. Florida Senior Living Pageant. Talk about causing a stir."

"Yeah, I get that. I'll try to be discreet. But you know Mrs. Mac. She's not exactly the cautious, retiring type."

"Well, do your best." The noise in the background grew louder, and Lucas said something I couldn't quite make out. I assumed he was talking to someone near him. "Look, Jackie, I have to go. I'm going to try to get home early tonight and come over to see you, but I'm not sure what's going on yet. I'll keep you posted."

"Where are you?" I trusted my boyfriend, but it wasn't like him to be out of touch like this, and we seldom went more than a day or two without seeing each other. I was curious, and given the uncertain state of the world, teetering on the brink of chaos as it was, I was more than a little worried.

He exhaled, the sound amplified by the phone. "I'm up at Carruthers. I came here to meet with Rafe, and then, of course, after the Reckoning today, I was returned here. We should be finished going over this information by this afternoon, and barring any more calls to broker deaths, I'll be home around dinner."

"Okay." I tried not to sound neglected and lonely, but I wasn't sure I'd succeeded.

"Hang in there, baby." Lucas' voice softened. "I love you. I miss you."

"I love you, too." I rushed to get out the words before he hung up. When there was nothing but emptiness on the other end, I clicked the phone off and stood up, stretching, glancing over at Mrs. Mac's house with trepidation. Keeping my eye on her without letting her know wasn't going to be easy, but I had an idea. It involved my neighbor's two favorite things: food and gossip.

"This was such a good idea." Mrs. Mac lifted up her glass of wine and grinned at us. "An old-fashioned girls' night! I haven't done this in . . ." She cast her eyes upwards, calculating. "Oh, Jackie, probably not since Maureen had her first stroke. That's been over five years. Way too long."

I smiled, thinking of Nana and how much fun she and Mrs. Mac had had together when they had both been healthy and spry. I missed my grandmother keenly, but sometimes the short period of time I'd lived with her here in this house seemed like it had happened to someone else. I'd been hurt and humiliated then, nursing a badly bruised heart after my near-miss of marrying an already-married man. Watching Nana struggle to recover from her stroke, only to succumb to a second one, had been painful, but I was grateful now that I'd been given the gift of those days with her.

"That's nothing." Charlie spoke up from across the table. "I've never done this before at all. Ever." She pointed at Mrs.

Mac next to her, my friend Nichelle in the chair alongside me and then at herself. "You know, hanging with girls."

To her credit, Nichelle just nodded. "Your friends were all guys?"

Charlie shook her head. "Nope. Didn't have any friends. Just my aunt and Reg, and all the people who came into the bar."

I tried to hide the stab of sympathy that hit my chest. I knew Charlie didn't want pity. But Mrs. Mac was never one to read the room and act accordingly, so she didn't bother hiding anything.

"Oh, honey, that's just not right. A woman needs girlfriends. Men have their uses, sure, and I'm one who likes a nice strong man, for sure, but girlfriends listen to your secrets. They hold your heart." She reached across the table and patted the young woman's hand. "But don't you worry, because now you've got us. Jackie and me, we've been tight for years. And now Nichelle's one of us, and you, too. We're like a little pack."

I giggled, sipping my wine. "Does that make you the alpha, Mrs. Mac?"

"Damn tootin." She lifted her glass in a toast. "I'm the oldest, and I'm the most experienced. So you should all listen to my advice. I'm . . . what's that word? Sage. That's it. I'm *sage*."

Next to me, Nichelle snorted. "Mrs. Mac, you know I love you, lady, but there are times when you're nuttier than an almond orchard."

That struck me as inordinately funny, and I nearly fell out of my chair, laughing. Nichelle joined me, one hand clutching at my arm. Charlie just looked at us, shaking her head.

"So what do we do now? Braid each other's hair and sing campfire songs?"

"No." Mrs. Mac tipped back her wine glass. "We talk about the real deal. Men. Our love lives. And who's doing who around the 'hood."

That got me giggling all over again. "Mrs. Mac, we live in an over-fifty-five community. The 'hood it is not."

She rolled her eyes. "You know what I mean. There's more action around here than there is in your typical college dorm. Did you know Lorna Peeks is sneaking into Arnie Coolidge's bed on the sly? She waits until nine o'clock because she figures all the neighbors are in bed, but not everyone retires after the re-run of *Lawrence Welk* on PBS. And you know that girl who comes in to do housecleaning for Saul Rupinski? I don't think she's just *changing* his sheets, if you know what I mean. His wife's been in long-term care at the memory unit at Spencer Creek for two years now. I guess a man gets lonely, huh?"

I cringed. Saul Rupinski was a sweet old man. His wife Dora had been the kind of dementia patient who simply faded away; she had never been belligerent or violent. It was only when she began to wander and Saul couldn't keep track of her that he'd reluctantly allowed her to be placed at Spencer Creek. Happily, the 'girl' Mrs. Mac had referenced was actually a good decade and a half older than me. If she was keeping a lonely man company . . . well, I wasn't going to throw stones.

Changing the subject subtly, I pushed the cheese platter her way. "Did you try this Danish bleu, Mrs. Mac? If you have it with the figs, it's divine."

"I'm so glad I'm done with breastfeeding." Nichelle reached for a piece of crusty bread and the cheese knife. "I can eat all the shit I want to and not worry about upsetting the baby's stomach. It's so freeing."

"If you're done nursing, must be time for another baby."

Mrs. Mac elbowed Charlie in the ribs, making her part of the joke. Charlie just frowned.

"Bite your tongue." Nichelle waved her hand. "I'm done. Three kiddos are just enough for me, thanks very much. Don't get me wrong, I love them all and I'd kill for them. But I'm ready to have my body back. Ready to have some grown-up conversation once a month or so."

"Aw, does that mean you're not going to bring Jack with you anymore when you stop by for deliveries? I miss my little guy." I'd delivered Nichelle's youngest child—on my front lawn, no less—when she'd gone into labor suddenly while dropping off blood for Lucas. She'd been so grateful for my help that she'd named the baby after me. I was touched and grateful; we'd become close friends since the first time we'd met on the day she delivered Lucas' initial batch of blood in Florida. That delivery had been my first clue that something was different about the new next-door neighbor.

Now Nichelle shook her head. "Nah, I couldn't keep him away from his Aunt Jackie. I'll bring him by every three days."

"What do you deliver every three days?" Charlie cocked her head at us, curious.

"Uh . . ." Mentally I scrambled. The cover story we'd used with Mrs. Mac as to why Lucas received a white Styrofoam cooler every few days had never come up in front of Nichelle. But now they all looked at me expectantly. I noticed Nichelle had raised one eyebrow. She and I never talked about why Lucas needed to have bags of blood so frequently, but I had a sense his wasn't the only odd delivery she made. She'd once mentioned that her company specialized in making discreet drop-offs to unusual clients.

"You can tell her the truth, Jackie." Mrs. Mac flung one

arm around Charlie's shoulders. "She's not going to judge him. Are you, honey?"

Now both of Nichelle's brows were practically in her hairline as she waited for my response. I went with the only answer that would satisfy at least one person in the room.

"Lucas has a condition which requires experimental medication. It has to be delivered right from the manufacturer, and Nichelle's company does that sort of thing." I didn't meet my friend's eyes. "But don't worry. It's not contagious or anything. He's fine."

Charlie lifted one shoulder. "Whatever. As long as he's not getting drugs or illegal body parts, it's cool with me. Live and let live, right?"

"Sure." I drained my wine and pushed back from the table. "Hey, look at that. Time to open a new bottle."

"Need help with that?" Nichelle's tone was amused but tolerant.

I reached for the corkscrew and shook my head. "Nope, I've got it." I scrambled for yet another change of subject. "So, Mrs. Mac, any more houses going up for sale? What's the latest on Augustus Row?"

"Two more this week. I hear he's been going door-to-door, handing out his card and putting the screws to anyone who's reluctant to think about listing with him. But I guess he won't have to worry about that when it comes to Norma Schmidt, huh? Did you hear she passed this morning?"

The bottle nearly slipped out of my hand. When Mrs. Mac had agreed to our girls' night with enthusiasm, I had assumed that word of our fellow Golden Rays resident's untimely death hadn't yet spread. But apparently I'd been mistaken.

"I didn't." Feigning ignorance was my best bet. If my

friend realized I'd known and hadn't said anything to *her*, I'd be in deep trouble.

"Yeah. She was pretty young and healthy, too. Here I was thinking she was my biggest competition in Ms. Florida Senior Living Pageant, and then she up and kicks off." Her face brightened. "Makes my odds even better, I guess." She cackled and winked at me. "Hey, Jackie, you know, maybe I offed her just to make sure I win this thing."

"Mrs. Mac!" My hand trembled a little as I tipped the bottle over her glass and then my own. "Don't even joke about that. Poor Norma. God rest her soul." I set down the wine and crossed myself in reflex. Mrs. Mac and Nichelle did the same, but Charlie just looked bored.

"Hey, relax, kiddo. She died of a heart attack. Although I guess I could have slipped her some digitalis or something. Does foxglove even grow in Florida, does anyone know?"

"Yep. It does." Charlie lifted her glass and took a drink of wine. "Aunt Val grew it in her garden, in back of the bar. She never let Uncle Reg touch it, though, because she was afraid it would hurt his heart."

"There you go." Mrs. Mac nodded. "There's where I got it. I convinced Charlie here to hook me up with the foxglove, and then I ground it up and put it in a cake I made for Norma. That's me. A brutal, cold-blooded killer."

I knew she was joking, but I also was aware, even if she was not, that Mrs. Schmidt's demise had actually been unnatural. Hearing her joke about it made me slightly ill.

"Mrs. Mac, when did you become so callous?" I glared at her. "I thought Norma Schmidt was your friend. How can you talk like that?"

"We were never close. She had that uppity attitude

because she used to play the piano in Europe. Called herself a concert pianist, but who knows? Maybe she just played bars and strip joints. There's no telling." Mrs. Mac grabbed a cracker and munched on it. "And when I was asked to be in the pageant this year, she got even worse. Told me I had no business participating. The nerve of her. Well, we see now who got the last laugh, huh? I'll wave to her with my scepter once I'm crowned next week."

I cringed, knowing my friend would regret her words when the truth came out. Or maybe not; she did seem pretty set against Mrs. Schmidt, even though I myself never remembered her being snooty or condescending. Still, the residents at Golden Rays had long memories—well, some of them did, anyway—and most had known each other for many years, some from even before they'd relocated here to sunny Florida. Maybe Mrs. Schmidt had mellowed by the time I'd made her acquaintance.

Charlie was observing with interest the exchange between my elderly friend and me, her eyes darting back and forth between us. "How long have you two known each other, anyway? When I first got here, I thought *she*—" She pointed at Mrs. Mac. "—was your grandma."

"No." Mrs. Mac smiled at me fondly and squeezed my hand. "But I've known Jackie here as long as her own grandmother did. Longer, I guess, since Maureen's passed and I'm still kicking."

"My Nana and Mrs. Mac were childhood friends," I explained. "They grew up together, and they even got married right around the same time."

Mrs. Mac nodded. "And when my sweet Billy was killed in Korea, Maureen adopted me into her own family. She was the best friend any woman could want. More like a sister."

"They actually moved down here at the same time." I remembered how sad I'd been when Nana had announced her intentions to relocate to Florida after I'd graduated from high school. But she and Mrs. Mac had been so excited when they'd bought neighboring houses, that I'd managed to put on a happy face for their benefit.

"Why didn't you and Jackie's Nana just live together?" Nichelle shifted, curling her legs up beneath her. "I always wondered that, ever since I've known you."

"Eh, Maureen and I were close, and we loved each other, but we also needed space. We were smart enough to know that. Also, we both had love lives, and that can get awkward, you know. Sometimes you're caught up in the heat of the moment and you don't notice the sock on the door. It might have been embarrassing."

I knew my face was red. "Mrs. Mac, really? I don't want to think about you and Nana having love lives, okay? As far as I know, you both went to Mass every morning and sat together to knit every night. That's my fantasy, anyway. Please don't destroy it."

"Oh, honey." She sighed. "Someday you're going to be my age, and I hope to heaven that you have the same kind of life I do. I hope you and Lucas are still sneaking between your houses, still getting it on in your car out in the driveway like you did that one night—"

"*What?*" Nichelle and Charlie both shrieked the word in unison. Charlie looked horrified, but Nichelle's face was alight with humor and anticipation.

I covered my eyes. "Mrs. Mac, I thought we agreed we'd never speak of that."

She blinked in pseudo-innocence. "Oh, I thought you'd told Nichelle about it. And if Charlie is going to be here for long, she's likely to hear about your shenanigans. Better we tell her than she finds out on the streets."

"Or we could just forget it ever happened and change the subject." I thought that was a good suggestion, but the rest of them acted as though I hadn't spoken.

"Dish us all the dirt, Mrs. Mac." Nichelle leaned forward, resting her chin in her hands. She shot me a withering glance. "I can't believe you didn't tell me about this, Jackie."

"Well, it was right before the Perfect Pecan Pie Festival, and I was just getting out of bed and making coffee, when Mrs. Ackers from down the street knocked on my back door—"

As if on cue, there was a sharp rap on the window of my kitchen door at the same time as it opened. Lucas stuck his head inside. "Hey. Is it safe for me to come in? I don't want to interrupt any girl stuff."

Nichelle made a shooing motion with her hand. "Go away. Mrs. Mac was about to tell us the story of you and Jackie in your car. You know, when you two got down and funky in the backseat."

"Actually, according to Mrs. Ackers, all of the good stuff went down in the front seat." Mrs. Mac put in helpfully.

"Oooooh, speaking of going *down . . .*" Nichelle laughed, a wicked glint in her eyes.

"Lucas, come inside." I stood up and grabbed his hand, pulling him toward me. It felt as though it had been a long time since the two of us had been together, even though it had been just three days. "Welcome home. Are you all right? Do you want something to drink?"

At the table behind me, Nichelle snorted. I ignored her

and stepped closer to my boyfriend. His arms slid around my waist, wrapping me in his warmth, and I rested my forehead on his shoulder.

"I missed you." Lucas's whisper brushed over my ear. "Come home with me?"

I only hesitated a moment. "Okay." Pressing my lips to his neck, just beneath his jaw, I inhaled, breathing in the scent I craved. "Just let me get rid of the peanut gallery." I paused. "Do you think Mrs. Mac will be okay if we leave her alone?"

He shrugged. "We'll be right next door, and Charlie is going to be here, even after Nichelle goes home. Everything will be fine."

"Just where do you think you're going?" Mrs. Mac called out as Lucas and I headed toward the door. "What about girls' night?"

"Go on without me." I tossed the words over my shoulder. "If you're just going to be talking about me anyway, I might as well leave you to it."

"She's not wrong." Mrs. Mac pursed her lips and nodded. "It'll be easier to tell you the story without her moaning and groaning all through it anyway." She waved at me. "Off you go. But do try to make it inside to lover boy's bedroom this time. Poor Mrs. Acker's heart probably wouldn't recover a second time."

I blew out a huff of breath. "Come on, Lucas. Let's go before she can mortify both of us more than she has."

"Have fun!" Mrs. Mac called out.

"Don't do anything I wouldn't do," Nichelle added. "Oh, wait . . . I think you already did."

Ignoring all of them, Lucas and I stepped outside into the night and fled for the sanctity of his silent house.

Chapter 3

"GOD, I MISSED you."

The minute we were inside his dark kitchen, Lucas swung me back against the door, framing my face with his wide hands and grinding his hips into mine. His mouth was on me, forcing my lips open as his tongue thrust inside me.

My own desire flared in response to his, and I raked my fingers through his hair, pulling him even closer. The tips of my breasts crushed into his chest, making me hyper-aware of each spot where our bodies touched. I felt as though I couldn't get close enough to him.

When I had to tear my mouth away to suck in a breath, Lucas tugged down the neckline of my shirt until it was below my boobs. With fingers that weren't quite steady, he curled his fingers into the cups of my bra and yanked them lower, nudging my breasts out into prominence.

"I missed you, too. And—ohhhhh." I ended on a moan as his mouth closed around my nipple. "I missed this, too. But are you okay? You're very . . . ummm . . ." My mind went blank as pleasure flooded my senses. "Intense."

"Yeah. I feel very . . . intense. I want you, baby. I want you now, and I want you hard. I want you to ride me rough when I take you right here."

He reached between us, fumbling with the button on my shorts while I unfastened his jeans. Lucas exhaled long when his hard shaft was free and in my hand.

"I need to taste you." Before I could take that in, Lucas grasped my wrists and lifted them up over my head. Holding himself in the other hand, he canted his hips, thrusting into me. I cried out, completely taken over by the assault of sensations, the pleasure of our joining. He pressed one insistent finger between us, rubbing the sensitive button of nerves that drove me over the edge of insanity.

As I arched, Lucas bent, fastening his mouth onto my nipple again and then, as I hit my peak, his teeth sank into the soft skin on the side of my breast. The sharp pain mingled with my climax, making both somehow more vivid. I could feel Lucas drinking from me, taking the strength that it seemed only I could give him, and it was exhilarating. It made me feel powerful and wildly feminine, like some kind of earth mother feeding her warrior.

When he wrenched away, I knew it had taken great effort for him to stop. He kissed me again, his tongue seeking mine. I tasted metal when he stroked against me, as though I'd bitten my lip.

"Jackie." Lucas skimmed his lips to my ear, his breath

warm on my neck even as he continued to move inside me. "I love you, baby."

"Love you, too." I barely ground out the words before he roared to his own orgasm, pushing into me until I came again, too, pulsing around him, every nerve ending alive and throbbing.

I slumped against Lucas, boneless in the wake of bliss. He caught me, and the two of us sank to the cool tile floor, our clothes still disheveled, pulled up or pushed out of the way. He held me on his lap as we caught our breath, coming down from the high of each other.

"You know, I hate it when you're gone," I murmured into his shirt. "But if this is how we celebrate your homecomings, maybe I can learn to adjust."

He shook a little, laughing. "Sorry about that. I guess I got a tad carried away. I was just so happy to see you. And after everything that went down this week, I think I needed a reminder of what's real and what's important."

"Things were rough at Carruthers?" I tried to keep the edge of hurt out of my voice. Usually, when Lucas made a trip up north to Harper Creek, the headquarters of Carruthers Initiative Institute, I went along with him. Now that I was officially a part-time agent, too, at the request of Cathryn Whitmore, I expected that our visits would become more frequent. I wasn't sure why Lucas had left without me this time.

As if he were ripping a page out of Cathryn's book—she could hear thoughts—Lucas sighed and rubbed small circles on my back. "I didn't know I was going to be up there for more than just a quick meeting with Rafe. I would've suggested you ride up with me, but with Charlie living with you, I wasn't sure it was a good idea for you to leave town just now."

"Ah." I nuzzled his neck. "But I thought one of the points of having Charlie stay with me was so that I could be free to concentrate on our saving-the-world gig. Didn't you say that? Or am I remembering it wrong?"

"That's what I said, yeah, but I thought maybe we should let her settle in and get used to everything before you took off. And since nothing's sure with her yet, leaving her alone in your house seemed a bit premature."

"You're probably right." I thought about my conversation with the younger woman earlier that day. "She doesn't seem to be very clear about what she wants to do. Except that she knows I have sucky knives and she wants to bring her own over." I sniffed. "Oh, and she has a car that's still over at her uncle's bar."

"That's something. Did she say anything about her plans?"

I shook my head. "Not really. Hell, I only got her to come out of the guest room today. I told her that she's welcome here as long as she wants to be with us, but I honestly have no idea about what's going on in her head. It's up to her, anyway. All we can do is offer her a safe place to be, but she's the one who has to decide if she wants to stay or if she plans to move on. Right?"

"Uh huh, I guess." Lucas frowned, a line forming between his eyes.

"Hey." I traced one finger over his forehead. "What aren't you telling me about the whole Charlie deal? I can tell you're holding something back."

"Not really." He caught my hand in his and brought my fingertips to his lips. "I don't know what it means, exactly. That's why I haven't said anything. Plus, I guess I was hoping you'd like Charlie so much that it wouldn't matter."

A chord of foreboding struck in my gut. "What wouldn't matter?"

Lucas kissed the center of my palm. "What the advocate for light said the day her uncle Reg died. During the Reckoning, when Charlie had gone off to call the paramedics, the advocate told me that Charlie was important. I thought he meant to the fight that's coming, but he said no." Absently, he rubbed his chin over my hair. "The advocate said that she was important to you and me. He used the word . . . bundle. He said Charlie's part of our bundle, the people who we're meant to watch over. She's supposed to be in our lives."

I smirked. "Is this some kind of test for us? To see if we're worthy to win the war against evil? Because Charlie's not exactly an easy person to have around. She's either holed up in a room alone, or she's sullen and sulky. Or she's complaining about something." Sniffing, I added, "And she insulted Nana's knives."

"Ah." Lucas was trying not to smile, I could tell. "Yeah, that's crossing a line, for sure. You didn't use one of Nana's knives on her after that, did you?"

"No." I let my eyes slide closed, relaxing against him. "Because they really aren't sharp enough to do any real damage. But still, it's the principle of the matter."

"She's definitely prickly." His arms tightened around me. "But I think that's because she's defensive. She might need a lot of affirmation before she trusts us enough to let us in. I get the feeling that the rest of the world hasn't done a great job of that. I mean, look at her history. Her parents run off before she's old enough to remember them. Her aunt, the only family she has, dies when she's a teenager. And then Reg is all she has. If you could've heard her crying that morning when he died . . . I know she's been stoic ever since, but I really think her heart is broken."

Now I felt guilty for all the uncharitable thoughts I'd been having. "If you're looking to convince me that I need to be more understanding . . . yeah, you're on the right track. I guess I can see how someone like Charlie might need two someones like us."

"And not just us." Lucas stroked one hand down my arm. "We have this whole set of people around us who would be happy to include her as one of our . . . tribe, I guess you could call it. Mrs. Mac, Nichelle, Mary and everyone at the diner . . . even Cathryn, Rafe and Nell."

That reminded me of something that had been niggling at the back of my mind. "If Charlie's going to be around a lot, though, how do we plan to explain the whole Carruthers situation? And you? I had to scramble to try to come up with a good reason for why Nichelle makes deliveries to you. If Charlie happens to walk in on you sucking down a bag of blood, you're going to have to do some fancy tap dancing."

"I thought about that. It shouldn't be a problem for the time being. I mean, I drink the blood over here, not at your house, and I can be discreet. The bigger issue is what to tell her when I get called to a Reckoning. That's one thing we can't control."

We both fell silent. I wasn't sure what was going on in Lucas's head, but I was thinking about how complicated our lives could potentially become, just by adding one person. I wasn't going to question the powers that be—not exactly—but at the same time, I had to wonder at the wisdom at tossing someone else into an already-dicey mix, at a time when all of our focus was supposed to be on saving the world.

"Cathryn had more information on the history of the Hive. That's one of the reasons she asked me to stay an extra couple of days up at Carruthers." Lucas stretched out his legs across the floor. "It's a pretty wild story."

"What we knew was already hard to swallow. I'm not sure I can handle anything even more bizarre."

"Then hold onto your hat. A Carruthers agent working undercover was able to catch one of the original hippies in a mostly-lucid moment, and this guy spilled his guts about how he and the rest of their group opened the interdimensional door. The leadership on the commune thought they were making contact with aliens who were going to help them achieve world peace. The plan was to start a fire—both literal and figurative—that was going to sweep over the world, destroying all the war and disunity, and then the aliens were going to take over and help us do things right." Lucas made air quotes with his fingers. "Of course, it really wasn't aliens they were contacting—"

"Do they even exist?" I interrupted.

Lucas wrinkled his brow at me. "What, aliens? How should I know?"

I lifted one shoulder. "Well, you're involved in the whole supernatural paranormal deal now, so I figured you might have some insight."

"I have no idea about that. None at all."

"Okay, then. Carry on." I rolled my hand, motioning for him to continue.

"So it turns out that instead of aliens, they really summoned . . . well, the demon, I guess. Or *demons*. The aging hippies still don't realize it, but putting together what we learned from Delia and what our investigators have unearthed, that seems to be what happened."

"Cathryn said before that all of the people involved in the original plan were either dead or demented, right? And they don't know the name of the leader?"

"Ah." Lucas held up one finger. "Yes, it's true that the men who did the ritual back in 1967 are in memory units or graves, but this one dude, in his brief time of clarity, was able to give our agent a name. A very important name, apparently." Lucas paused, and I assumed it was for dramatic effect. "Donald Parcy."

I wrinkled my nose. "Seriously? The big bad we've been hunting all this time is named *Donald*?"

Lucas cocked his head. "Why? You wanted him to have a more threatening name?"

"Hell, yeah. Donald is your uncle, or the old man next door who yells when you run through his roses. Donald isn't the guy who's going to bring the world to the brink of horrific war and bloodshed."

"I guess when his parents named him, they didn't foresee his role in the apocalypse." Lucas nudged me forward. "My ass is going numb. We need to get off the floor." He snapped his pants and buckled his belt again.

"Sorry." I stood up, pausing to fix my shirt and my bra where Lucas had pulled them out of the way earlier, in his rush to get to me and re-buttoning my shorts. "So have they found out where this guy is right now? Is he still alive?"

Lucas opened the fridge and retrieved two bottles of beer. "He is. He's living in a nursing home outside San Francisco, since he had a stroke about five years ago. Cathryn has a Carruthers contact watching him, just to see who goes to visit him. We don't know if the Hive plans to use him, or if he was just a means to end back then. There was something kind of funny, though."

"Funny ha-ha, or funny weird?" I took a long swig of the beer Lucas handed to me.

"Funny ironic. It turns out that these people had their timing all wrong. They were fifty years off, which is why their plan didn't work. They were able to start the process, but I guess these things are affected by the position of the stars or something . . . because it didn't succeed. Only one entity slipped through before the door closed."

A chill ran down my spine. It was one matter to talk about the upcoming end times in abstract terms, but I knew from personal experience that things were going to get messy and terrifying. I'd had a front-row seat to a preview of coming attractions when we'd tried to summon a deceased double agent earlier this autumn. Instead of appearing as a non-corporeal spirit, as Cathryn had planned, Delia had decided to enter me and possess me for a short time. It hadn't been a pleasant experience, to say the least, and when Lucas had sent her back to the gray place—some kind of limbo, I assumed—she hadn't gone easily. I still woke up sometimes with the memory of her screams in my head.

"And just where is this, uh, *entity* now?" I glanced over my shoulder as though it might be lurking in the dark yard.

Lucas rubbed his forehead. "We're not sure, but Rafe has a theory that if it's a demon, it might be possessing a series of bodies, which means it may have been a shit ton of different people over the last fifty years. That's why he wanted my help, to go over a list of potential men and women who may have been the demon's hosts."

I shivered again. "That means it could be anybody. People who work for Carruthers, anyone here in our neighborhood . . . we'd never know."

"Yeah." Lucas nodded. "Cathryn thinks she'd be able to tell if someone who was possessed was close to us up at Harper Creek, probably, by probing the minds, but she's been fooled before. We know that. And she can't exactly be near all of us all the time to check on the people we come in contact with on a daily basis. Nell and Zoe are working on increasing security, first at the Carruthers headquarters and then for all of us involved." He hesitated a beat before continuing. "And this means that we're probably going to have to move up there sooner rather than later."

Deep down, I'd known this was a possibility. While Cathryn had assured us that we wouldn't have to relocate in order to be part-time Carruthers agents, we'd all realized that eventually, when the real battle drew near, we'd have to hunker down in one safe place. I had been trying to avoid thinking about that, but now . . . I felt nauseated.

"What're we going to do about everyone else? I understand that we have to be with the rest of the team, but what about my parents and my brothers? My nieces and nephews, and Leesa and Harold?" Tears sprang to my eyes. "And Mrs. Mac, and Nichelle, and Jack—"

"Jackie, I get it." Lucas laid a hand on my shoulder. "I know what you mean. We'll do whatever we can to keep them safe. But ultimately, the best way to do that is for us to focus on stopping the Hive. If we can do that, we'll not only help our family and friends, we'll be able to save the whole damn world." He gathered me close. "Try not to worry, okay? It's not something we have to do right away. I just want us to be . . .

prepared."

I buried my face in his neck and took deep breaths, leaning into the one source of strength I could trust, and tried to push away the images of our world plunging into madness.

Chapter 4

"STOP THE PRESSES. I have news."

Slowly and with great effort, I raised my eyes from the book in front of me on the table, blinking at Mrs. Mac as she sailed into my kitchen. I was having trouble coming alive this morning; after our hot and heavy session against the kitchen door and the sobering discussion that followed, Lucas and I had eventually wandered back to my house and my bed. By that time, Nichelle and Mrs. Mac had gone home and Charlie had retired to the guest room. The relative privacy had apparently inspired us, since we'd made love again, this time with more care and finesse, our awareness of precious time ticking away informing our every touch and caress.

As a result, though, my ass was dragging this morning. Two cups of high test coffee hadn't even touch my grogginess.

And seeing Mrs. Mac's face, bright and wide awake, wasn't helping right now.

"I can't stop the presses. The presses haven't even begun yet." I lifted the coffee mug and wondered distractedly what had happened to my last gulp. Had I taken it? I couldn't remember.

"Oh, come on, sleepy head. Rise and shine and sparkle." Dragging out the chair opposite of mine, she dropped down into it heavily. "Did someone stay up too late last night with her lover boy?"

I scowled. "*Someone* doesn't want to talk about it before she has another cup of coffee." I stood up, reached for the pot and tipped it over my cup. "I'd offer you coffee, but it appears I'm out."

Mrs. Mac waved her hand. "I don't want any, thanks. I've been awake for hours. I had to meet with my voice coach this morning to work on my number for the pageant."

Kill me now. Almost against my will, I bit the bullet and asked the question. "What is it that you're planning to sing? And who's this voice teacher? I haven't heard you mention having anyone helping you."

"I'm singing the love song from *South Pacific*. We were thinking about something more contemporary and current, but Karen feels that my voice is more suited to something timeless and classic. And she's not a teacher—she's a coach," Mrs. Mac corrected. "She's a lovely woman who was the Ms. Florida Senior Living Queen five years ago. Now she helps other contestants, since she's been through it and knows the ropes. I was just lucky I nabbed her services before the competition did."

"Aha." I nodded and took another slug of coffee. "She's in

high demand, huh? What's her name?"

"Karen Folgers. She lives over on the other side of Golden Rays, so it was a real race for me to get to her before that bitch Rachael Hilton did."

"Mrs. Mac." I shook my head. "You're supposed to show grace and dignity as a pageant contestant, aren't you? That's not exactly the Ms. Florida Senior Living Queen way."

"No, it totally is." She nodded, unrepentant. "This pageant has a reputation for being dog-eat-dog. There's no room for namby pamby playing around. We're very cutthroat."

"Nice. Who's this Rachael Hilton?" Apparently the third cup of coffee was the charm, as I was beginning to slowly come alive.

"She's the other singer in the pageant. And she's even worse than Norma Schmidt was when it comes to being snooty."

News of Mrs. Schmidt's unnatural cause of death had not yet been made public. I had a hunch that the police were afraid of hysterical senior citizens calling into the tip line every time they saw a shadow move. They probably hoped to figure out who'd killed her before they had to issue a general warning to the community.

"Well, good for you for hiring the voice coach first." I wondered what the going rate was for teaching an elderly woman to carry a tune. I hoped she wasn't fleecing Mrs. Mac, but then again, the poor teacher likely deserved hazardous duty pay for taking her on. "Oh, and what was your good news? I'm mostly awake now. You can tell me."

"Excellent." She beamed at me. "I got you a job."

My brows drew together. "Did I need another job? I thought overseeing a diner, writing a cookbook and starting up a catering company were going to keep me pretty busy." *Not to mention saving the world during my downtime . . .*

"No, silly. I mean, I got you a catering gig. You know, you're just starting out, and I realize it's going to take you a little while to make your name in this business. So I just happened to be at the pageant meeting this morning, dropping off my music for next week, and I heard them saying their regular caterer was going to be on vacation, so they didn't know what to do. They were talking about bringing in food from the grocery store for the pre-pageant meal—can you imagine that?"

"I really can't." I had an inkling that I knew where this was going. I wasn't certain I was going to like it.

"Of course, I told them that my best friend and honorary granddaughter was an excellent cook and a caterer, too, and that I was sure you'd be happy to jump in and handle the brunch."

"Mrs. Mac, I'm not really certain that I want to . . . did you say brunch? That's the pre-pageant meal?"

She shrugged. "Yep. You know some of these old girls, they can't eat so late. The pageant starts at noon, and the brunch is usually underway by nine."

"Oh." I took another sip of coffee. "I'm not sure that brunch is really in my wheelhouse, Mrs. Mac. I figured I'd be starting out by doing things like appetizers at cocktail parties and maybe making lunches or dinners for birthday picnics. I wouldn't even know quite how to create a brunch menu."

"I can help."

I jumped a little, startling at the sound of Charlie's voice in the doorway from the hall. She was dressed in a clean pair of jeans and a shirt that actually almost fit her, instead of her standard baggy number, and I thought with surprise that she really was a very pretty girl.

"I know how to do a brunch. That's what I did for my final project at culinary school. I planned and executed a celebration breakfast for a morning wedding." She cast me a sideways look that was just a tad smug. "And I got an A on that project, by the way."

"See that?" Mrs. Mac clapped her hands together. "Perfect. So you and Charlie can work together and make this happen. The pageant committee would like to have a menu to approve by the end of the day. I'll leave all the information right here." She dropped a slim pile of papers on the table and then rose from her chair. "Now, I have to run home to get my vocal exercises in, or Karen will be cross with me. Tootles, girls!"

After the door slammed shut behind her, I turned to face Charlie. "I hope you know what you just got us into, kiddo. Cooking for a passel of old people before a senior citizen beauty pageant? And making brunch for them?" Shaking my head, I sighed. "They might eat *us* alive."

To my amazement, Charlie smiled. I hadn't seen her yet without that perpetual scowl, and in my shock, I might have gaped, mouth open.

"It'll be fine. We'll do omelets and stuffed French toast, and then bacon and homemade sausage as our meats. Oh!" Her eyebrows shot up, and I swore her eyes actually sparkled. "And blintzes! Those are perfect for brunch. Everyone loves blintzes."

She sounded so elated that I couldn't help joining in with her, just a little. "And some kind of potato, too. Home fries or hash browns?"

Charlie narrowed her eyes, considering. "Do you have a deep fryer?"

"At the diner, yes. So you're leaning toward hash browns?"

"I was thinking, why not both? We could make them ahead of time, so that's not too much on-site work. Is there a kitchen at the venue, or do we need to worry about an electric skillet? And do you have chafing dishes and warming trays yet? Oh, maybe a coffee station, too. Wouldn't that be cool? I have recipes for making natural flavored creamers. Or some of those tea blends you're always playing with."

I wasn't sure I'd heard Charlie string together this many words in the entire five days since I'd known her. Apparently we'd just learned that the key to unlocking her personality was brunch for old people.

"I have chafing dishes, and we can get warming trays from the diner. I don't even know where they're having this shin-dig, so I'm not sure about the kitchen. I guess I'll have to call and find out numbers and then give them a bid on everything." I flipped through the pile of papers Mrs. Mac had left behind. "I never thought that I'd have only a week to prep my first catering job, you know? I figured I would set everything up for the business, but I didn't expect to actually book any clients until after . . ." I stopped, realizing what I'd been about to say. *I didn't plan to cater anything until I was sure the world was going to keep going 'round and 'round.*

"Until after what?" Charlie cocked her head and regarded me curiously.

"After the holidays." Lucas came to my rescue, entering the kitchen from behind Charlie and making a beeline for the coffee pot. "Jackie didn't want to put any pressure on herself with her family and her friends coming down here for Christmas. But I'm thinking I missed something, sleeping in late this morning. What's going on?" He lifted the now-empty pot, shaking it and frowning.

I jumped up out of my chair and took the pot out of his hand. “Sorry about that. I was a coffee hog this morning. Sit down, and I’ll make more while Charlie tells you what she’s gotten us into.” I kissed his cheek as I passed by. “Oh, you’re going to love this.”

Lucas did, indeed, get quite a laugh out of the idea that Charlie and I were going to cater brunch for the Ms. Florida Senior Living Pageant. But once he got over the initial humor of the idea, he jumped on the bandwagon with Charlie, the two of them coming up with ever-more grandiose ideas for how to make this the best brunch ever served to people least likely to remember it.

They were in the middle of listing all the possible omelet ingredients when a familiar expression passed over his face. I knew what it meant, and I knew what came next. Catching Charlie by the hand, I dragged her out of the kitchen.

“The trays for the chafing dishes are in the garage. Come help me pull them out so we can see if we need to order more.”

“Now?” She frowned at me, confused. “But we were still finishing this list.”

“Yes, now.” I was insistent, pushing her ahead of me out the door that led to the garage as I gave Lucas wide eyes over my shoulder, watching him until, as I’d expected, he vanished into thin air. “Lucas has to get ready for an appointment this morning, anyway. And if we need to get more trays, I want to order them so they'll get here on time."

Once we were safely on the other side of the door, I relaxed, and the two of us pulled out boxes and began counting supplies. We determined that between what I had on hand and what the diner had, we were going to have plenty of serving dishes.

"I haven't ordered plates, glasses or silverware yet," I mused as we boxed up everything again. "As I said, I didn't plan to start so soon. I figured if I had to, I could borrow them from the diner, but there's no way I can do that during breakfast. It's one of the busiest times of the day at Leone's."

Charlie gnawed the corner of her lip. "I can get us what we need from the Stinker. All those dishes are just sitting there since it's been closed . . . we might as well put them to good use." She took a deep breath. "If you'll give me a ride over there this afternoon, we can load them into your car and into mine. It's probably a good idea for me to have some transportation, so I can do some legwork for next week, right?"

I was conscious of the need to tread carefully. As Lucas had pointed out to me, Charlie was much more fragile than her tough exterior showed. Thinking of myself at her age and imagining what it would have been like to navigate life without anyone to help, I made a deliberate decision and nodded.

"Absolutely. It would be a big help for me if you could handle some of the shopping and maybe even negotiate what we're going to charge them, once we have an estimate of our costs. Having your own car here is a good idea."

"All right." Charlie leaned against a plastic tote, crossing her arms in front of her small chest. "I got an email yesterday. It was from Uncle Reg's lawyer. I guess he did have one, after all." She flickered a glance at me before resuming her staring contest with the cement floor. "He left me the bar. He left me *everything*. I can't believe it, but he did."

"Charlie." If she were anyone else, I'd have pulled her into a comforting hug. "Wow. That's huge."

"I guess he didn't have anyone else to leave them to." She was retreating, trying to play this off, but I wasn't going to let her.

"He left his whole life's work to you, Charlie. Don't underestimate how important that is." I ventured one hand out to squeeze her arm. "If Reg went to the trouble of making a will, it means he thought about this. You're not his heir by default. He chose you."

To my shock, her eyes filled with tears. "He was a good guy," she whispered. "I didn't always let him know I knew that, but he was. He could've kicked me out when Aunt Val died. He didn't have any real ties to me. But he didn't. He kept me."

This time I didn't fight the urge to hug. Gathering her close, I smoothed Charlie's spikey black hair under my hand. "The longer you live, one of the things you learn is that we choose the people we love. I have a family up north, and I love them dearly, but I also have my family down here: Lucas and Mrs. Mac, Nichelle and her kids, Mary and everyone at Leone's. I love them just as much." I paused a moment. "You can choose to be part of us, too. I know you probably feel like we were thrust upon you, that we all found each other by accident, but I know that there's no such thing as coincidence or happenstance. Everything happens for a reason."

Charlie nodded, but she didn't speak.

"We haven't known each other very long, of course, and you might think we're all a bunch of whackadoodles. We are, actually." I pulled back a little and winked at her. "But we're very loyal whackadoodles, and if you give us a chance, we won't let you down. Not on purpose, anyway."

Charlie swallowed, her throat working as she stepped back. I knew she needed a little distance now, and I was willing to give it to her.

"I don't know what I'm going to do yet. I'm not sure I want to run the bar, not without Reg. And I'm not ready to go back there to live." She shuddered slightly.

"You don't have to," I assured her. "Even if you decide to open the bar again and give it a go, you can stay here as long as you want. I was serious when I told you that yesterday."

She focused on some distant spot over my shoulder. "Thank you. Thank you for . . . giving me a place to be."

I mirrored her stance, folding my arms over my chest and speaking with measured words. "You're welcome. Now let's go get your car and the dishes. We need to get moving on this job. Fast."

Chapter 5

THE STINKER, THE late Reg Landon's bar, wasn't nearly as seedy as I'd pictured it to be. The exterior was campy, with the fish painted on the bricks, but everything was neat and well-maintained. Inside, it was the same story. A wide variety fishing paraphernalia, both contemporary and vintage, hung on the walls. The bar was clean, and the tables and chairs were relatively new.

Even the kitchen was in good shape. As I watched Charlie move around the room, opening cabinets and taking out plates, saucers and cups, I wondered how much of its pristine condition was her doing. She definitely knew her way around.

We'd come in through the front of the bar, and I noticed that she avoided the part of the kitchen that led to the pantry and freezer. Judging a couple of telltale stains and some medical litter, I realized that must have been where her uncle had collapsed and died. I didn't blame her for not wanting to linger there.

We worked together quickly to pack up the dishes before we loaded first her car—a blue compact that was definitely used, but seemed to be in good shape—and then mine. I stayed downstairs to give her some privacy while she packed some more clothes and other essentials. Once she was finished, we didn't waste any time heading back to my house, Charlie following me in her car.

We were just pulling into the driveway when my cell rang. I grinned when I saw the caller ID screen as I answered the call.

"Is this the beauteous Jackie O'Brien?" Rafe's voice held its perpetual teasing note.

"I don't know about beauteous, but it's me." I shut off the car and opened the driver's side door. "What's up, Rafe? Aren't you supposed to be saving the world instead of flirting with middle-aged women?"

He laughed. "You're not middle-aged, gorgeous. You're barely old enough to be my big sister."

I rolled my eyes, but I couldn't stop the pleased smile from creeping over my face. Rafe was a good friend, someone I'd felt comfortable with from the first moment we met. Getting to know both him and his girlfriend, Nell, was one of the bright spots in our connection to Carruthers.

"Flattery will get you nowhere. What can I do for you?"

"It's more like what I can do for you. Or rather, what Nell can do for you. Are you home?"

I glanced back to where Charlie was climbing out of her car and beginning to unload boxes. "Just got here. Why?"

"Because you're about to get company. Nell and I are

about five minutes away. That cool?"

"Uh . . ." I cast a quick glance over to the house next door. Lucas's car was there, but that didn't mean he'd returned from the Reckoning that had called him away earlier. "Yeah. Of course. I always enjoy seeing you two. Just so you're aware, though, I have a houseguest. Or . . . a boarder." I wasn't quite sure what to call Charlie yet. "And she's not aware of the extra-curricular activities that go on around all of you guys."

"Ah, is that the chick Lucas brought home after the Reckoning?" Rafe sounded amused. "He told us that story. Nell informed him that he was damned lucky you're so tolerant and accepting."

"Have I mentioned how much I love your girlfriend?" Nell Massler was not the warm and cuddly type. One of the most powerful witches who'd ever walked the earth, she tended to exist in a constant state of barely-controlled energy, and her eyes were usually guarded. But she loved Rafe, and she'd allowed Lucas and me to get close enough that the four of us had formed a close-knit circle of friendship.

"Get in line, baby. This woman's all mine." I heard the muffled sound of a voice on the other side of the phone, and Rafe chuckled again. "Don't worry. We'll be cool around the civilian. We just need to chat, and there's some business we have to take care of, but we can be subtle, I promise."

"I trust you." And I did. "Not sure if Lucas is around, but I'll be happy to see you."

"Awesome. Be there in a flash, babe." He disconnected, and I tucked the phone back in my pocket as I wondered what was this was all about.

Charlie paused near the trunk of her car. "Everything okay?" She'd resumed her serious, distant stance, but she'd lost the sullenness. I could live with that.

"Yes. A couple of friends are in the area, and they're going to stop by." I briefly considered telling her a little about Rafe and Nell but decided against it. She'd see them soon enough for herself.

We'd just finished toting in the last box of dishes when a 1967 black Chevy Impala turned slowly into my driveway. Charlie's eyes went wide.

"Oh, my God. That car is gorgeous." Her mouth dropped open.

I smirked. "Wait until you see the guy driving it."

The door opened on the driver's side, and Rafe Brooks emerged, looking every bit the sexy man beast he was. His dark hair was its typical hot mess, just begging a woman to run her fingers through it. Green eyes smoldered in a near-perfect face. And the body? Let's just say when Rafe moved, every-one around him was more than a little turned on. His black T-shirt strained over the broad chest and muscled arms, ta-pering to a narrow waist where jeans hugged both his perfect ass and steel thighs. When I saw him, all I could think was *sex personified*. He had the goods, and watching him, it was clear he knew how to use them, too.

"Oh . . . my . . . God." Charlie gripped my arm, her breath coming now in little puffs. "Please, tell me he's single. Tell me he's not gay. Tell me he's not an asshole."

I laughed softly. "Not gay. Definitely not an asshole. He's one of the best men I've ever met, outside Lucas." I gave a little sigh. "But sadly for you, also not single. Check out the passen-ger side of the car."

As though she could hear us from all the way down at the end of the driveway, Nell climbed out of the Impala with an amused expression on her striking face. If Rafe had the type of magnetism that drew everyone toward him, Nell was the opposite end of the spectrum. Her air of banked power made most people hesitate to get too close. She was beautiful, even if it was in an unexpected way: her jet black hair set off the palest skin I'd ever seen among the living. But it was the huge, bright blue eyes that made passers-by often stop and stare.

"Hey, pretty lady." Rafe reached me, wrapping me in a tight hug that spoke of our close friendship. I also felt somehow safer and more relaxed when he was nearby. Perhaps that was part of his supernatural power: Rafe was a mind manipulator. He could influence the direction of thoughts, the strength of emotions . . . and he could even play with memory and the perception of time.

"This is a very nice surprise." I tiptoed to kiss his cheek, rough with stubble, and then turned to greet Nell, too, hugging her. She allowed it, although her response was much subtler than Rafe's was.

"It's always good to see you, Jackie." Her voice was low and thrummed with energy. "Sorry for the short notice. We were on our way back from a visit with Rafe's grandparents when Cathryn asked us to detour here."

I glanced up at Rafe, frowning, but he only gave his head a little shake as he smiled down at the young woman standing next to me, still gaping at him.

"Hey. I'm Rafe Brooks." He held out one large hand. "You must be Charlie. Glad to meet you."

As if in a trance, Charlie placed her small fingers in his grip. "Yeah. Charlie."

"And this is my girlfriend, Nell."

As though it physically hurt her to do it, Charlie ripped

her eyes away from Rafe and managed a semblance of a smile at the other woman. "Hey. Nice to meet you."

Nell nodded, one side of her mouth quirked up in her habitual half-smile. "You, too. Rafe and I work with Lucas." She slid her gaze to me. "And sometimes Jackie."

Charlie's eyebrows drew together. "Oh. You mean at his other job? The one he has to go away for sometimes?"

"Exactly." Rafe grinned. "Consulting. We . . . consult." He slung a friendly arm around my neck. "And we're also very good friends. We love Jackie. It doesn't hurt that she's a damn good cook, too."

"Yeah, yeah. I know the hard truth. You only love me for my food." I pretended to pout, and Rafe smacked a kiss on my cheek.

"Aw, don't be silly. We love you for all your other wonderful qualities, too."

Shaking my head, I ducked under his arm. "Come on. Let's go inside before the neighbors start talking about me two-timing Lucas with the hot younger man who's hanging around."

The kitchen was nearly filled with boxes, and Nell raised one eyebrow. "Are you moving, Jackie?"

I snorted. "Hardly." Our eyes met, and I knew what we were both thinking. Lucas and I might be moving soon, but it wouldn't involve packing boxes. Wherever we went with Carruthers, we'd all be traveling light.

"No," I continued after a beat. "Charlie and I have a catering gig next week, and these are the dishes."

"What're you catering?" Rafe's eyes crinkled in amusement. "The early bird special?" Rafe never got tired of laughing at the fact that Lucas and I lived in a retirement community. It was an endless source of teasing for him.

I grimaced. "You're not far off. We're doing the brunch before the Ms. Florida Senior Living Pageant."

Rafe threw back his head, chortling. Even Nell's smile was wide as she elbowed him in the ribs. "Stop. I think she's serious."

"I am." I could hear the resignation in my tone. "Mrs. Mac is a contestant, and she volunteered us to cater it." Hooking a thumb toward Charlie, I narrowed my eyes. "And this one agreed that we could do it."

"Oh, I gotta be there for that. Can you get us tickets? Seriously. I want to support Mrs. Mac." Rafe twined his fingers with Nell's. "We can do that, can't we? When is the pageant?"

"Next week." I shook my head. "But it's a long way to drive for something like this. You don't have to do it."

"Jackie, babe, I wouldn't miss it for the world." Rafe winked. "Matter of fact, is Mrs. Mac around? I think I'll go over and talk to her about hooking us up with tickets." He amped up the wattage on his killer smile, turning it on Charlie. "Want to walk over there with me? I'd love to hear about what you're planning to serve for the brunch."

I wasn't sure whether or not Rafe was using his mind manipulation on Charlie. At this point, I was fairly certain that all he'd have to do was crook his finger and she'd follow him anywhere, even without that extra intervention. Her eyes had the luminous glow of a girl in the thrall of a serious crush as they walked out of the kitchen.

"And there goes my lover, with his latest conquest." Nell sounded resigned, if slightly amused. "He just can't seem to help himself."

I sighed. "He doesn't see anyone but you, Nell. You're his

forever."

"I know." Nell had never struck me as the jealous type, and that wasn't any different now. "But don't you ever wonder what that would be like, to have that kind of natural charisma? To attract people of both sexes, wherever you went? Rafe just has this . . . something . . . that makes everyone want to be closer to him." She bit her bottom lip. "I've always seemed to have had the opposite effect. The one that makes people want to stay away."

"You're just reserved. There's nothing wrong with that." I leaned my back against the edge of the kitchen counter. "Something's up, isn't it? Why did Cathryn asked you to stop here?"

"It wasn't quite that surprising." Nell shrugged. "We figured we'd be making the trip down here sooner or later, but Cathryn suggested it made sense to do it now, since we were passing fairly close by on our way back from King. She wants us to increase your protections here." She hesitated. "And I think she wanted us to check out Charlie, too. You know—with us not being certain what form that demon might take or whose body he could be borrowing, any time someone new enters our lives, we have to be cautious."

I hadn't even thought about the fact that Charlie could have been a vehicle for the demon from the Hive to gain access to Lucas and me. "You don't really think she is, do you?"

"Honestly? I can't tell for sure, but I don't get a vibe, and I don't think Rafe does, either. Cathryn would be the final word, of course. But until she can get down here, I think you're safe. Especially considering the advocate for light mentioned her to Lucas."

"He told you about that?"

Nell nodded. "He wanted us to have the whole story, just in case. She seems all right, though. I don't think she'd be drooling after Rafe so obviously if she were demon trying to fly under the radar."

"You may be right." Although I had a hunch even demons would probably find Rafe irresistible. "I haven't noticed anything off. She's sort of difficult sometimes."

"Aren't we all, at times? We'll keep an open mind and see what happens." Nell stood in the center of the kitchen, turning in a slow circle as she surveyed the room. "What I need to add here isn't anything complicated, but it should keep all the nasties at bay, at least for the time being."

"If we can do this, why do we need to think about the possibility of moving away? I thought the only reason for us to gather was to make sure we're safe." I'd been trying to think of a way around leaving Palm Dunes. The idea of abandoning my friends at a time when we all could be facing the end of days made me feel ill.

"What I can do has a limited lifespan, and it might not work on everything. Plus it can't protect from humans who mean you harm, and we know the Hive often uses them." Nell closed her eyes, raised her hands into the air. Everything around us shimmered for a moment before she lowered her arms and looked at me.

"I can work with this. No one's been trying to infiltrate here that I can perceive, so I'll do a basic boundary spell and then add a few extra bells and whistles. It'll allow you both to go about your lives without any worries."

"How will we know if someone's disturbed your boundary? Will they be physically kept from intruding? Or will there be some kind of alarm?" I tried to imagine what that might sound like and wondered whether or not my usual daily intruders—Mrs. Mac and other neighbors—would accidentally set it off. That could get dicey.

"You won't know, and neither will they or anyone else nearby. Certainly no one who's . . . typical. But I will know." Her eyes met mine, and somehow the calm assurance and confidence I saw there made me feel better. Although I'd never really seen her in action, outside of the summoning spell she'd done the day we'd called for Delia, I had a healthy respect for Nell's abilities.

"Thank you, Nell." I laid one hand on her arm. "I appreciate this, and I know Lucas does, too."

"Just doing my job." She offered me a smile. "We want you and Lucas to be safe. When everything is said and done, we're a team, and we're all integral to making sure we can stop the Hive. I have a vested interest in keeping you both alive and well."

"Still." I looked out the window, over to Mrs. Mac's house. Rafe and Charlie had gone inside, and I imagined the three of them laughing together as they visited. Mrs. Mac was probably regaling them with stories of the pageant. "The longer we can stay down here, the better I feel. I'm worried about leaving everyone I love, you know? It feels like I'm choosing my own safety over theirs."

"You're not, though. You're making the hard choice to keep them safe by putting yourself at risk." She followed my gaze out the window, pensive, and I wondered what was crossing her mind. "I had a similar conversation with Rafe on our way here. He's understandably worried about his grandparents, once everything starts going down. He's been trying to work out some place where they could go, and he wanted to talk to them about making plans." Nell shook her head. "But his gram absolutely refused. She said there's no way she's being shuffled off just when she might be needed."

"The difference is that Rafe's grandparents are in the loop. They know what we're potentially facing, and they can make an informed decision. The people I love have no idea. Lucas and I will go away, and we'll have to make up some kind of cover story to explain why. If everything works out and we win, then everything's okay. We come home, and life goes on. But if it doesn't . . ." A lump rose in my throat. "If it doesn't, then at some point our friends and family will be in danger. They could be . . . destroyed, and they'll never know that we left to try to save them."

"I'm sorry, Jackie." Nell didn't argue with me. She never sugarcoated the hard things in life. "I wish it were different. But all we can do is our damnedest to destroy this thing once and for all. We have to give it everything we've got. But meanwhile, trust that all of us—including Cathryn—are working as hard as we can so that you and Lucas can stay here—and be safe."

"I know. Thank you for that." I inhaled deeply. "Do you need anything from me for this spell? Or should I get out of your way?"

She shook her head. "No. Stay with me, please. You have a very comforting aura, Jackie. You . . . put me at ease, which means the magic flows better."

One side of my mouth curved up. "I guess that's something. Okay, then, I'll just sit here and be comforting." I maneuvered around a box of dishes and dragged out a kitchen chair. "Tell me if there's anything else I can do to help."

Nell closed her eyes again. This time when she raised her

hands, I could sense something stronger flowing over us both. If I'd been pressed, I might have described a purple color, although I might not have been able to say precisely what it was.

It didn't take long before she stopped, sighed and took the seat across from me. Her face was peaceful.

"That should do it. If there's any kind of disturbance, I'll be in touch right away, and we—"

The door opened, and Lucas came into the kitchen, frowning as he glanced around the room. If he was surprised about the boxes or even Nell's presence, he didn't give any indication. Instead his eyes sought mine, and my heart sank when I saw the worry there.

"Jackie, where's Mrs. Mac?"

I pointed out the window. "She's at her house. Rafe and Charlie are over there with her. Why, what's wrong?"

Lucas ran a hand through his hair. "There's been another murder. Another pageant contestant is dead. She was strangled, just like Mrs. Schmidt."

My mouth went dry. "Who was it?"

He gripped the back of a kitchen chair and stared down at me. "Her name was Rachael Hilton."

Chapter 6

"HOW COULD YOU not tell me?" Mrs. Mac covered her face with both hands and asked the same question she had been repeating for the past thirty minutes. "You let me say all those horrible things about poor sweet Norma . . . and all the time, you knew she'd been *murdered*? And now Rachael." She glared first at Lucas and then at me. "And remind me again how you knew Norma's death was unnatural?"

Lucas sighed. "I have a source of information. But I couldn't say anything to you until there were more details available."

"So I was in danger this whole time and neither of you cared about that?" She crossed her arms over her chest and glared at us. "Let's face it. If someone is bumping off the contestants most likely to win the Ms. Florida Senior Living crown, I'm the one who's next on the list."

"We've been watching out for you, Mrs. Mac. Of course we have." I spread my hands. "But we didn't want to alarm you or make you worry before we were certain about what was going on." I glanced over my shoulder at Charlie, who was sitting silently with us at Mrs. Mac's table. "That's why Lucas and I have been trying to make sure you're never alone."

"Hmph." The elderly lady remained unconvinced. "I still can't believe you didn't tell me."

I had a hunch that being out of the information loop was the bigger issue here for my friend. She hated being the last to know about anything, and that probably outweighed any fear she might have had about the threat to her very life.

Rafe and Nell, wise as they were, had beat a hasty retreat after Lucas and I had broken the news about Rachael Hilton to Mrs. Mac. Just before they pulled away, Rafe had rolled down his window.

"We'll try to be back next week for the pageant. And the brunch." His grin had broadened. "Wouldn't miss that for the world. Good luck, beautiful."

"You're assuming that any of the contestants are going to live long enough to compete." My stomach was still roiling from the news. "This is serious, Rafe. I know it's not a threat to the world at large, like what you and Nell are seeing every day, but it's a threat to *our* world."

"I know." He'd gotten serious right away. Bless his heart, Rafe loved Mrs. Mac, too. I knew he was worried. "But as Lucas pointed out, we don't see any clear motive for rubbing out the would-be beauty queens. This might just be coincidence, a series of breaking and enterings that went bad. Lock your doors at night, and watch out for all of your neighbors."

He'd winked at me. "To tell you the truth, I'd bet on Mrs. Mac against any thief trying to steal her stuff. And if she ran into someone who wanted to keep her from that competition? No contest at all. She wants this crown bad."

Rafe was right, I knew. At this moment, Mrs. Mac was more embarrassed about the way she'd talked in the wake of Norma's death than she was fearful for her life. And with her next words, she revealed her biggest worry.

"You don't think they'll cancel the pageant, do you?" She laid one small, blue-veined hand over her heart. "I've been waiting my whole life to do this. They just can't take the chance away from me. Not now when it's so close I can practically taste it."

Lucas shook his head. "From what I hear, the pageant connection is just one theory the police are considering. It could still be a coincidence."

"Really?" I was skeptical. "Three contestants dead, and that's a coincidence?"

"*Three*?" Mrs. Mac glanced from me to Lucas. "Who's the third? Norma, Rachael . . .?"

"The first one was Judy Conrad," Lucas replied. "Although the police didn't consider her death a homicide until they took another look at it in the wake of Mrs. Schmidt and Mrs. Hilton being murdered, apparently they're no longer sure that the fall that killed her was accidental."

"Mrs. Mac." I leaned forward and covered her hand with mine. "Has there been anyone in the pageant who seems especially, uh, intense about winning? Anyone who might be crazy enough to try to bump off the competition if she was worried it was the only way she might be able to win?"

My friend gazed back at me, misery etched on her lined

face. "Just one." Her bottom lip trembled a little. "Only . . . me."

I sat back in my chair. "What're you saying?" Surely this wasn't a confession. I knew Mrs. Mac could take things a bit too far at times, but she wasn't a murderer.

"I'm just saying that all the other contestants look at this pageant as a lark. Most of them were winners back in the day. They all had crowns when they were young and spry. To them, this is nothing more than a community event to raise money for charity. I'm the only one who's never been a beauty queen. I'm the only one who cares about winning." Tears swam in her eyes. "But I swear, I didn't do it. I didn't kill Norma or Rachel or Judy. I wouldn't even think of it."

"Of course you didn't." I patted her shoulder. "No one thinks you're a suspect. And there's nothing wrong with wanting to win, Mrs. Mac. You shouldn't beat yourself up for that."

"I don't." She shook her head. "I blame my father. If he'd only have let me compete when I was younger, I wouldn't care so much now." She heaved out a deep breath. "But there's no use in crying over spilled milk, is there?" She squared her small shoulders. "All right, then. What do we do now? How can we catch this terrible murderer? You'll use me as bait, of course."

My mouth opened to protest this idea, but before I could say anything, the doorbell rang. Lucas jumped to his feet, as though to protect us all, but Mrs. Mac only shook her head.

"Calm down. I don't expect the killer to stand on niceties like doorbells if he—or she—is coming to do me in." She stood up and headed for the living room to answer the door, with the three of us trailing in her wake.

The man who stood on Mrs. Mac's small front porch was tall and thin. His blond hair was nearly colorless and slicked back from a narrow face. He was dressed impeccably in a suit that fit him like a glove and a tie knotted perfectly at his neck. This dude would've appeared to fit in on Wall Street or on the sidewalks of Manhattan, but here in Palm Dunes, where dressing up for men meant a fresh Hawaiian shirt and clean shorts, he seemed to be out of place.

"Good afternoon." He offered Mrs. Mac his hand, and when she took it, he turned it and lifted the back to his lips in a weird imitation of the old courtly gesture. "You must be Mrs. MacConnelly. Pleasure to make your acquaintance. I'm—"

"Oh, I know who you are." Mrs. Mac yanked her fingers away and put her hands on her hips. "You're that snake oil salesman who's been sweet-talking all the ladies into selling their homes. I knew it was just a matter of time before you made your way around to this part of Golden Rays. Well, buddy, you're out of luck here. I'm staying in my house until they carry me out feet first. So go sell your story somewhere else, Mr. Augustus Row."

Ah. So this was the real estate agent Mrs. Mac had been ranting about a couple of weeks back, I realized. I'd forgotten all about it, what with the pageant, the murders and the impending doom of the world ending.

"Ma'am, you have me all wrong." Augustus Row smiled, and I would have sworn charm was oozing from his pores. But it wasn't the kind that Rafe exuded; this guy made me feel as though I needed a shower. "I don't want to try to talk you into anything. I only stopped to offer my condolences in the wake of these shocking losses. I saw that you, too, are in the running for the Ms. Florida Senior Living crown, and I wanted to tell you how sorry I was to hear of the untimely passing of Mrs. Schmidt and Mrs. Hilton." He flicked open one hand

and offered Mrs. Mac a small cream-colored square of paper. “And if you feel that in light of these murders, you no longer wish to live in a neighborhood where innocent women aren’t safe, I’m more than happy to assist you in finding a new, safer community.”

“She’s plenty safe here.” I stepped up, glaring at the man. “Mrs. Mac is surrounded by friends and neighbors who have her back twenty-four/seven. She’s not going to be coerced into giving up the home she loves.”

Augustus glanced from me to Lucas to Charlie, all of us forming a united backing to our friend. An expression I couldn’t decipher skittered across his face.

“How refreshing to see such a show of support.” He beamed at Mrs. Mac, but like just about everything else involving this guy, it felt fake. Phony. “You’re a very lucky woman.”

“Yes, I am.” She gripped the door knob and began easing the door closed. “So if you’ll excuse us, I don’t think you have any more business here. As a matter of fact, I don’t think you have any more business in this whole neighborhood. I think you should hit the road, buddy.” Mrs. Mac swung the door forward, slamming it in the surprised face of Augustus Row.

For a moment, we were all silent. And then Mrs. Mac turned toward us, her eyes sparkling with renewed determination.

“All right now. We have a lot to do, and not much time to make it all happen.” She pointed at Lucas. “*You* need to come up with an effective plan for catching the sicko who’s bumping off pageant contestants.” Next her finger moved to Charlie and me. “And *you* two need to finalize all the plans for the brunch.”

I quirked one eyebrow. “And just what are you going to be up to while the rest of us are on these missions, Mrs. Mac?”

She smiled at me, and it was a sight both terrifying and wonderful to behold. "I'll be busy rehearsing my number for the pageant. I have a crown to win."

"Mrs. Mac just called to report that she is going to bed. The house is locked up, and Charlie's going to be awake for a while. Apparently she's still working on the menu and the pricing for the brunch." Dropping my cell on the coffee table, I sank into the couch next to Lucas. "So all is well in the world. For now, anyway."

"Good to hear." Lucas drew me close to his side, snaking his arm around my waist. "Suggesting that Charlie stay with Mrs. Mac until we're sure she's safe was an excellent idea, too. I feel better knowing they're looking out for each other."

"And the fact that it gives us a little more privacy?" I snuggled against his solid warmth. "How does that make you feel?"

"Hmmm. Maybe I should show you that, instead of trying to tell you." Lucas shifted to face me more fully, nudging my chin up so that he could reach my lips. His kiss was soft and relaxed at first, a gentle touch, and then he deepened it, urging me to open to him.

With a groan that vibrated into my mouth, he gripped my hips and swung me around to straddle his body, never breaking our kiss. I laughed against his lips and pressed my breasts into his chest, thinking how glad I was to have this little bit of time to ourselves after the craziness of the day. We hadn't figured out what was happening with what the local press had dubbed the Pageant Princess murders (privately, I thought it was quite a stretch to refer to these contestants as princesses, but I assumed the need for alliteration trounced the desire for strict accuracy). But on the positive side of things, the unexpected visit from Augustus Row had given Mrs. Mac a renewed determination to win the pageant and had distracted her from being upset with Lucas and me.

I felt a little safer, too, knowing that Nell's spell was firmly in place. Even though we hadn't had any threats from the supernatural quarter yet, it was comforting to be able to trust that we had one less worry.

And one less worry meant I could take this brief moment to enjoy my boyfriend without guilt or second-guessing myself. Grinding my core against the ridge of his burgeoning desire, I trailed kisses along his jaw.

"What was that?" There was strain in Lucas's voice. "Is someone knocking?"

"Mmmmm . . ." I nuzzled his neck. "Just my heart. You're making it pound."

"No, really." Lucas eased me away, and I caught the spark of concern in his eye. "Someone's knocking at the door. It could be Mrs. Mac or Charlie."

Without any further ado, he dumped me onto the couch cushion and stood up, making for the front door. I scowled at his departing back. Couldn't we catch a freaking break? Just one evening without any interruptions?

As if to underscore the answer to that question, my phone began to buzz from its spot on the coffee table. Muttering to myself, I grabbed it and answered.

"Yes? What?"

"Jackie? It's Nell. Is everything all right there? I got a ping on the protection spell." She spoke with quiet urgency. "Where are you? Is Lucas all right?"

Fear spiked in my heart. "Yeah, he's with me. Shit. Someone just knocked on the door, and . . ." I trailed off as Lucas came back into the living room. Just in front of him stood a familiar woman. Long black hair fell in a silken curtain around her slender body, and ice-blue eyes regarded me with cautious resignation.

The night I'd seen her at the Perfect Pecan Pie Festival, she'd been dressed in a long skirt and a flowing jacket. Tonight, she wore fitted jeans in a deep blue wash and a black scoop necked long-sleeved shirt. Even so, there was no mistaking her identity.

"It's Veronica," I breathed into the telephone. "She's here in my house. With Lucas and me. You need to tell Cathryn."

"Jackie." Veronica held out one hand, palm toward me, as though to ask that I slow my words. "I'm not here to do anyone any harm. I promise. I came at Lucas's request." She glanced up at him. "Please. Tell my granddaughter there is no need to fear me. I'm on your side."

With my eyes glued to the vision in front of me, I spoke slowly into the phone. "Nell, she says—"

"I heard her." Nell was tense. "Unfortunately, none of us are in any position to take her words for truth. I'm going to call Cathryn now, and then . . . I'll be in touch. Keep your phone nearby and call me if you need us."

"Okay," I answered, but the click on the other end told me that Nell had disconnected before I'd spoken.

"May I sit down?" She indicated the chair alongside the sofa, but she didn't move until I'd nodded.

"Please." As if by instinct, I moved a little bit further away.

Lucas came around the couch and sat down, putting himself between Veronica and me. He took my hand in his, and I shivered at the chill in his skin.

"First, Jackie, I must apologize for not introducing myself when we met at the Pecan Pie Festival. It was rude. But at that time, I was not yet ready to make myself known." She turned her attention to Lucas. "I was not yet ready to face Lucas."

"But now you are?" I squeezed his hand. "And are you also, uh, ready to give us some explanations? Like what you did to him that night back in New Jersey, and why?"

"Of course. I'll be happy to tell you everything." She answered me, but she didn't look away from Lucas. "You may not like everything I say, but I promise, I will not lie or evade."

"Hmmm." I couldn't help staring at Veronica. It wasn't every day that I met a vampire—well, a complete vampire, anyway; Lucas was only a half-vamp. Or so we assumed. But Veronica had an otherworldliness about her that I suspected had more to do with her long life than with any mystical powers she might possess.

She smiled at me then, and I nearly fell off my seat. The full force of her attention was overwhelming. Tilting her head, she ran the tip of her tongue over her red lips.

"I should probably warn you, Jackie. My many-times over great granddaughter inherited her gift for hearing thoughts from me. I'm quite proficient at blocking them, but just now, it is important that I'm at full alert, to make sure we're not disturbed by anyone who means us harm or overheard by any spies. So I'm able to hear you. I'm sorry about that, but it's for all of our safety." She paused and then added, "Primarily yours. At this point in my existence, I'm nearly invincible. You two are not."

"We got it. Don't think anything we don't want you to know." Lucas nodded.

"Not you, darling." Veronica lifted her shoulder in small Gallic shrug. "As I turned you, I am not privy to your thoughts. It's some sort of built-in measure of privacy, I assume, although I have no idea for sure."

"Let's start there." Lucas opened his free hand, the one that wasn't still clutching mine. "Let's begin with why you, uh, turned me. I want to know all the answers. I think I deserve to know them."

"Of course you do. But the story doesn't begin with you, dear one. With any luck and some hard-fought battles, it won't end with you, either. But in order for you to understand everything fully, I would ask that you indulge me. I'd like to share a little bit of history before we, as you might say, get to the meat of it."

Lucas glanced at me, and I nodded. "I've always been someone who wants the whole story. So please, by all means. Tell us everything from the very beginning."

"Excellent." She clasped her hands around one denim-covered knee. "Before I begin, I wonder if we might have some tea. I'm especially partial to that lavender blend you've been brewing lately, Jackie. Do you mind?"

My first instinct was to ask her how she knew about my favorite herbal tea, but I decided it wasn't important at the moment. Instead I nodded and stood up.

"Let's adjourn to the kitchen. I'll put on the kettle."

Chapter 7

"THIS IS EXACTLY what I needed tonight." Veronica lifted the delicate china cup to her perfect lips and took a sip, closing her eyes. "Thank you, Jackie, for sharing it with me. I don't want to jump ahead of myself, but I've been keeping my eye on you both for some time, for your protection. I'll admit that when you brew this tea, I've been nearly salivating. It's excellent."

It wasn't every day that a centuries-old vampire complimented my tea, so I decided I was perfectly within my rights to be a little proud and preen a bit.

"It's actually my own blend. I'm picky about tea, and I don't like most of the store-bought brands. I'm considering adding custom-blended teas to our catering menu."

"A wonderful idea." She nodded and then carefully set down her cup on the saucer and took a deep breath. Beside me, Lucas tensed slightly. We'd been waiting so long for answers to the mystery that had been his life the past few years. Now, both of us were afraid of that truth.

"My story begins, as does that of every living thing, with my birth. Mine took place in Scotland, in the year 1628."

My breath caught. I'd surmised that Veronica had lived a long time, but the reality of nearly four hundred years of life—or something like it—was startling to consider when it was confirmed to me. Veronica's lips twitched.

"I've aged well, I like to think."

I nodded fervently, and she continued.

"We weren't an especially wealthy or well-known family. My father had pulled himself up from the merchant class to the edges of aristocracy, but even so, we weren't special as a family. However, by the time I could speak, it was clear that there was something different about me. I had a gift, although there were times when I was unsure if it was instead a curse.

"As I've told you, I have the gift of mind-hearing. When I was very young, I wouldn't have described it as such; I merely knew things. My parents and our servants became used to it in time. There were no secrets around me. I didn't know how to control the ability, but I did learn discretion, thanks to my mother. She never punished me or showed fear of me, but she counseled me to be careful about where and how I shared what I knew. She told me that knowledge was currency, and I had to learn to spend it wisely. So I understood early the value of holding my tongue and biding my time.

"I was the oldest of five children, and before I was even a full decade old, there was talk of whom I would marry. My parents realized that they had to be cagey about whatever match I made. If my gift was discovered, there was the real chance that I might be burned as a witch. Aside from the obvious downside of that possibility for me, it would irreparably harm my family's reputation and destroy my siblings' chance of happiness and prosperity.

"My father had a connection, a distant cousin who had met and married a woman from the coast of Spain. The woman had been the only child and heir of a wealthy family, and so my father's cousin had moved to Spain after his marriage to become the don of the family's villa. This cousin had a son a little older than me, and after a few years of correspondence, the marriage was arranged. Along with my parents, I traveled to their villa, and I married Benito Carruthers."

Lucas snorted. "Quite a name."

Veronica laughed, and as on the night we'd first met, I was reminded of the tinkling of bells. "It was indeed, and my sisters teased me about it unmercifully before I left Scotland for my wedding. They called him 'little Benny'. It made me cross, because I was terrified of living so far from my family and of marrying a man I'd never met. But the first moment I laid eyes on Benito, I fell in love."

My heart thudded. No matter the context, everyone loved a love story, and I was no different. The way Veronica spoke, I could picture the nervous young girl, so far from her home and country, meeting the man whom she was bound to marry. It sounded like a romance novel.

"It *was* very much like a romance novel." Veronica smiled at me. "Benito was tall and well-built, with his mother's black hair and dark eyes. He lifted my hand to his lips, and at the last minute, he turned it over and pressed a kiss to the palm. I was . . . smitten." She sighed, and I found myself sighing right along with her. Next to me, Lucas cleared his throat.

"Yes, of course. I'm sorry, Lucas. You must indulge an old woman's memories." She winked at me. "Suffice it to say that although our marriage had been arranged like the most practical business deal, for us it was a love match from the beginning. It helped that I could easily anticipate Benito's intentions and desires; pleasing him was not difficult when I could hear what he was thinking. When my parents left me there and returned to Scotland, they were satisfied that they had done the very best they could have for me. By the end of our honeymoon, I was already with child.

"Our son Adriano was born before our first wedding anniversary. He was strong and healthy, and my life was complete. I couldn't imagine ever being happier. Benito's parents loved me as though I were their own daughter, my husband desired me above all others, and now I had gifted him with a son. We were blessed beyond measure."

I was suddenly struck with sadness, because I realized that this story could not have a happily-ever-after ending. The fact that Veronica sat here in front of us, a supernatural creature, made that fact plain. I dreaded the next part of her tale. Part of me wanted to cry out for her stop, to let it end where she'd just paused.

"Oh, Jackie. I wish that, too. I wish that I'd given my husband a dozen more healthy children and grown old with him in our beautiful home. But wishing for something doesn't make it so, and pretending can't change the past." Veronica laid a hand on my arm. I jumped; she was so oddly cold, and then there was something else, too . . . something slightly predatory, as when I'd been near a panther at the zoo. I didn't feel that I was in danger, but I wasn't perhaps entirely safe, either.

If she noticed my reaction, she didn't let on.

"When Adriano was just shy of a year old, some business associates of my father-in-law came to visit us at the villa. They were three brothers, Spaniards, and two were perfectly normal, joining us for meals and walks along the beach. But the third one, we were told, had recently been ill. He wasn't contagious, but he could not walk with us, and he didn't come to dinner. When the men met to discuss business, he kept to the shadows, speaking only now and then. Such was his avoidance of people that I didn't actually meet him until they'd been at the house for a few days, but when I did . . . well, Jackie, your reaction to my touch just then was not unlike my own feeling."

I swallowed hard and nodded.

"Of course, I had the additional benefit—or curse—of being able to hear the man's thoughts. What I heard frightened me beyond belief. This man—his name was Diego del Fuego—his cravings were terrifying. He wanted . . . blood. He wanted to drink from the servants, male and female, and he wanted my Benito. He was curbing his desires, but just barely. And then he met me, and after that, *I* was who and what Diego wanted. What he craved. He would do anything to have me. I could hear, deep in the recesses of his twisted mind, the beginnings of a plan that would spell the destruction of my family.

"His brothers didn't know what he was, though perhaps they had suspicions, but thus far, he'd kept his, ah, activities to the shadows. He'd drunk prostitutes and thieves and animals. But now he was in company again, and the pounding of his want was like a beat in my own chest. I knew that it would only be a matter of time before he gave into it.

"But what could I do? If I had told Benito . . . why, he would have thought that I was insane. Or perhaps he would have believed that I was a witch, as my parents had feared might happen. There was no cause for anyone else to suspect that Diego was anything more than an invalid visitor. I thought, and I cried, and I prayed. I went to our priest, and in the sanctity of the confessional, I shared my suspicions, never letting on how I'd come by these fears. The priest told me that I was letting my imagination run away with me and suggested it was time for me to have another child.

"If it had only been that easy! Finally, with no other recourse, I confronted Diego in his room late one night. I told him what I knew, and I begged him, on the life of my child and his brothers, to go away and leave us before it was too late. I swore that I would never tell anyone, and I tried to convince him that despite this misfortune that had befallen him, there was still good deep within his soul. I suggested that he go to the church and request help. I thought perhaps a priest with an open mind could help him.

"But I'd underestimated his lust for my blood. Diego listened to me speak, and once he realized my gift, my ability—because how else would I have known for certain what he was?—then he wanted me all the more. So he made me an offer. My life, my blood, and ultimately, my companionship, for the lives of my husband, my in-laws and my son."

Veronica fell back against her chair and covered her eyes. My heart was breaking along with hers, and I wanted to reach out and comfort her. But I stayed still.

"I protested and I bargained, but in the end, Diego stayed firm. He gave me one day to decide. If I came to him the next night and gave myself willingly, he would never touch anyone else at the villa. If I did not, he would decimate every living creature there. Man, woman and child."

She took a deep breath. "Of course, there was no real choice. I promised I would come to him that next night, but I begged for one concession. It was bad enough that I would be forced to leave my family, but I couldn't bear the thought of Benito and my son believing that I had left them of my own free will. So I wanted Diego to make it look as though I'd been taken. Kidnapped. It happened, after all; there were pirates who looted that coast, and it wouldn't have been out of the question for a band of them to take a young woman they might've spied walking on the beach.

"Diego recognized that this would actually be in his best interest as well, so he agreed. The next day, he shared with his brothers and my father-in-law that while walking late at night, he'd seen the silhouette of a ship off the shore. He planted that seed. The next night was meant to be the final evening of their visit, and he presented the men with a bottle of expensive port. He'd drugged it, so that all the men fell into a deep sleep. Once they were all passed out, I went to Diego."

Veronica's face was a mask of pain. Four centuries had not dulled the agony of the decision that she'd been forced to make.

"Together we tore apart my room, broke a window and for the piece de resistance, he cut my wrist and spread blood over the sill and bed. I was still bleeding when I bent over the crib of my sleeping son and kissed him for the last time. And then I touched my lips to my husband's, breathed a good-bye to my Benito. After that . . . Diego dragged me outside, down to the beach. Among the rocks, he laid me down and drank me."

I touched my face, surprised to feel tears on my cheek. "How did you go on? How could you leave them?"

She stared out the window into the dark night. "I had no choice. Once I had been turned, I knew I could never return to my family. I was too different. And Diego held that threat over me, too. As long as Benito was alive, as long as my son lived, I owed Diego all of me. He was jealous, and he could be cruel. I had planned to get away from him as soon as I could and kill myself, but I'd underestimated how difficult it is to destroy a vampire. And I worried, too, that if I were gone, Diego might go back and kill my family. So I stayed alive . . . or whatever I was, whatever I am now, in order to give my husband and my son the best chance at life that I could."

"And they really believed you'd been taken by pirates?" Lucas spoke for the first time in a while.

Veronica nodded. "As coincidence would have it, there really was a band of privateers not far from the coast that night, and they raided a nearby island town. It wasn't a stretch to assume they'd also taken me. Diego had left a trail for the men to follow, and he'd robbed the villa of some valuable pieces, as well. He made quite the show of helping the men look for me, although of course he told them he was still too weak to be out in the sun. Meanwhile, I was hiding at a house he'd rented several hours' journey from my home. After a few days, Diego and his brothers left the villa. His brothers went their way, and Diego separated from them. From that time on, we were together."

"You must have hated him," I breathed. *I* hated him.

"In the beginning, I did. But one thing you must know about a long life is that hate will consume you. After the first hundred years, I began to let it go." Veronica traced the wood grain on my kitchen table. "Benito . . . he never married again. I'd thought he would. He was young and virile and wealthy, but he grieved for me the rest of his days. My son grew up well, raised by his father and his grandparents. When he was in his early twenties, he made a journey to Scotland to meet his mother's family—my parents and my sisters and brothers. I'd kept track of him all this time, but I couldn't approach him as long as Benito was alive or his parents were near enough that they might recognize me. I followed Adriano to Scotland, though—I'd been back before that, to check on my family there—and it was in my homeland that I spoke to my son for the first time in twenty years. I pretended to be a stranger he met on the stage, and we only talked of small, mundane topics, but still—I was with him. I could watch his eyes, search his face for bits of Benito and myself.

"I was so proud of him. I stayed nearby as long as he was visiting, never close enough again to be seen, but just watching . . . I saw him meet the girl who would become his wife. He married a lovely Scottish girl and took her back to Spain. I heard eventually of the births of my grandchildren." She sniffed. "They named their first daughter Veronica. I cried for days when I learned that."

"What about your life with Diego?" Lucas leaned forward. "Did you drink? Was the transition difficult for you? When did you leave him?"

Veronica's brow wrinkled. "The transition was . . . painful, and full of sorrow. Not only had I lost my family and my humanity, in those days we assumed that vampires were all evil, a scourge, and despicable to God. So I lost the Church as well. I was too afraid to approach even the church yard. And yes, I drank. In the early days, I followed Diego's lead. He brought me to evil men and women, to those about to die . . . I had to drink. The craving drove me mad at first. But I never took a life without crying for days afterwards, even those lives that were about to end anyway. Before too long, those were the only humans I would drink: those on the brink of death. I told myself that I was easing their way into the inevitable."

Lucas said something low, under his breath. If Veronica heard him, she didn't give any sign.

"As for my life with Diego, it was different than anything I'd ever known. We traveled extensively. We couldn't stay in the same place for long. We changed our appearance often. Diego was fascinated with my ability to hear minds, which had stayed with me into vampirehood, and he liked to use me in that capacity to suss out business opportunities or chances for us to drink without suspicion. He still traveled with his brothers now and then, though not frequently. He told them that he had a wife and that we lived in Italy. About twenty years after he'd turned me, he paid a man a great sum of money to report news of his death—and that of his so-called wife—to his brothers. It was necessary, you see, because they were aging and he was not."

"How did Diego become a vampire?" I was curious; it seemed that he must have been fairly new to the life when he'd changed Veronica, since his brothers had been alive.

She pressed her lips together. "That is his story to tell, and not mine. All I can tell you is that it happened one night when he had been riding home very late, along a dark and lonely road, and he never knew for sure the name or face of the man who'd sired him into this life. Or this non-life. He was found wandering and delirious the next day and taken home, where they feared he would die. But apparently the vampire who made him slipped into his bedroom and delivered the bad news, that he was now a blood-drinker. That happened only about six months before Diego and his brothers visited our villa."

"Is Diego . . . still alive?" I thought of the vampire stories I'd read. In those, sometimes vampires went underground for decades, when the undead life just became too much for them.

"He is." Veronica hesitated and then shook her head. "More on that later. For now, I'll tell you that the day my son passed from this life, I left Diego. I told him that I had fulfilled my obligation to him, kept my promise, and now I was going to live on my own."

"But what about the rest of your family? Your grandchildren? Didn't you worry Diego might kill them if you abandoned him?"

She smiled. "As odd as it sounds, Diego is a man of his word. That night, when I'd begged him to go away and leave us alone and we'd made our bargain, he'd accepted my blood in exchange for that of Benito and Adriano. In his mind, my grandchildren, my siblings' offspring . . . they were of no matter. I'd kept my end of the deal, and so would he."

"What did you do? Where did you go?"

She stretched out her arms. "Oh, dear girl, where *didn't* I go? After all that time, I was finally free. I went all over Europe, down into Africa, into China and India . . . eventually, I made my way to the New World. My family was among the early settlers in this lovely state. I kept my eye on them in St. Augustine, and then I visited now and then once they'd established the home base at Harper Creek. For years, I had to continue my practice of drinking from the dying, but the longer I was a vampire, the more I began to learn. I was eventually able to take little drinks, without killing a human. And once those marvelous places called blood banks were invented, I never was forced to drink from a living person again."

"How many did you turn over the centuries?" Lucas was terse as he stared at Veronica. "How many lives did you turn inside out? How many blood suckers like you did you create?"

She pursed her lips, her eyes wide and frigid as she returned his glare. "One. In nearly four hundred years, I turned one person. Just you, Lucas. Only you."

For a few minutes, the air between them crackled with tension. Lucas was wound so tight that I feared he might leap onto her, and Veronica was like a cat, watchful and waiting.

Lucas slumped back in his seat, closing his eyes. "So now we know your story. Can you fast-forward through the colonial era, the Revolution and the antebellum years and maybe bring us into the twenty-first century?"

"Of course." Veronica didn't respond to his baiting with anything but a slight smile. "But you have to understand, as I pointed out, that I had been keeping my eye on my family over the years. I had seen that my own gift had been passed on through the generations—and I had also realized that in some of my descendants, that ability had morphed a little. Some had other talents that were related to my mind hearing, even they weren't exactly the same. And before long, those in my family with these gifts began to seek out others like them. When the Institute was created in the late eighteen hundreds, I was very pleased. I thought my mother, particularly, would have liked this idea, as she'd been one of the most practical and accepting people I'd ever known.

"Now and then, I used my connections to help the Institute. I'd send information, or I'd nudge someone along. It let me pretend that I was part of them, even though of course to this modern group of Carruthers, I was nothing more than a footnote in the family history.

"And then . . . something happened. I was in California in the late 1960's. Well, everyone who was anyone spent some time there during those years." Veronica looked a little embarrassed; I had the sense that if she could have blushed, she might have been doing just that. "I was a flower child. A hippie. I hung out in Haight-Asbury, I participated in sit-ins . . . and the music! Oh, God, the music. Janis Joplin. Jefferson Airplane. The Grateful Dead. The Mamas and the Papas. I heard them all, and I even knew some of them fairly well." She smirked a little. "I had a lot of money by then, and no one else had two cents to rub together. I funded quite a lot of concerts, road trips and protests."

I tried to imagine this beautiful, exotic woman with granny glasses and flowers in her hair. "It must have been incredible to live through that time."

"It was. Oh, I've been part of so many ages . . . it can make me tired to remember, but there was hope in those days. Even though we were horribly cynical, it was a different sort of cynicism. We liked to talk a lot, but deep down, we really thought we could end war. Save the world." She met my eyes. "Unfortunately, in some people, that hope and belief evolved into arrogance—a misplaced sense that it was our duty to do whatever was necessary to change society. People twisted our message in horrible ways, and the things that happened . . . well, it sickened me.

"But none more so than the day I heard through the grapevine about a commune north of San Francisco. A friend of mine told me a story about a group of men and women who had gone a step further than the rest of us. These people had been delving into the supernatural. They'd been studying the paranormal. Some of the leadership believed they'd been called to open the door to another world—a world of peace and serenity, a world without war. But they also knew that this couldn't happen without bloodshed. And they were willing to make that happen."

This was beginning to sound eerily familiar. "The Hive. That was—what was his name? Donald?"

Lucas nodded. "Donald Parcy. You were part of that?"

She rolled her eyes, impatient. "I wasn't part of it. I was trying to stop it. Most people who heard about this group figured they were crazy. But being who and what I was, and knowing what I did, I realized that they could be inviting into the world an evil that they could neither anticipate nor control."

"What did you do?" I gripped the edge of the table. It was like something out of a movie . . . except, I reminded myself, it was real.

"I got to the commune as fast as I could, and I insinuated myself into the leadership. I used my mind hearing to get a closer look at their plans. And then I realized something: they were way off on their timing. They were using some faulty texts as the basis for the date of their ritual, and it was going to be wrong. I began to relax, because I thought, well, nothing will happen and then eventually they'll all just fall away. They'll forget about it.

"Still, just to be on the safe side, I hung around until the day of ritual came. Only five of them were allowed to take part, but I listened in on their minds so I knew what was happening. Everything went according to their plans, until it didn't.

They were so disappointed that I also felt sorry for them. I was about to duck away and disappear, when I heard . . . something. It was a voice, and not a human one. A shot of pure power ran through the five men, and it was strong enough that even just hearing it through the minds, I was knocked off my feet. The pain . . . it was incredible."

"What did the voice say?" I held tight to Lucas's hand, not even aware that my nails were biting into his palm.

"It wasn't a language they could understand, but I could and did. It was ancient. And it was insistent. The voice was telling them, *Open the door. Open the door.* Over and over, pushing and demanding. I lay on the ground there in the woods, and I curled in on myself. I hadn't been in that much misery since the day Diego had turned me. But I didn't know what to do.

"Finally, there was some kind of a snap, as though a string had broken or a wall had crumbled. I couldn't explain it. The pain eased, the voice stopped, and I was just getting to my feet when something went through me, like the bitterest wind you could ever imagine. It was cold, and it was ugly, and I was more frightened than I'd been the entire time, because I realized that whatever they had let into our world was now free."

"That was the demon." Lucas sighed and leaned his forehead into his hand. "They opened the door and let it escape."

"Exactly." Veronica glanced at me and then back at Lucas. "That day, I didn't know what to do next. I wanted to give chase, but I didn't even know how to start pursuing an entity I could neither see nor hear. I started toward the five men, but the closer I got to them . . ." She massaged her forehead as though feeling the ache from that day. "Chaos. Complete and utter chaos in their brains. Whatever had been unleashed had unhinged them all. They were babbling madmen. The rest of the commune didn't know what was going on, but once the men began to stagger out of the clearing, there was screaming, and people ran as far away as they could. I tried to help, but it was no use."

"What did you do?"

"I thought about going to Carruthers with the story, but there wasn't anything that they could do any more than I could. I realized all I could do was wait and see. For a solid year, I stayed in northern California, waiting and watching for I didn't know what. But nothing happened. The Summer of Love ended, the age of the hippies began to end, and it seemed I'd been worried for nothing. I couldn't perceive anything out of the ordinary."

"Until . . .?" Lucas prompted.

She inhaled. "Until Carruthers had a case that involved a local senator and a friend of his who was going to run for office. The would-be candidate had a girlfriend who was murdered, and the Institute was hired to prove that this man was innocent. In the course of the investigation, they ran up against something . . . unexpected. Something that was more than they'd ever seen before.

"I'd just happened to be nearby because Cathryn was struggling. Of all of my descendants—and there are quite a lot of them now—she is one of my favorites. She reminds me of myself, I think: we share a gift, and although she seems to be controlled and almost frigid, deep down, she's much more vulnerable than you might think." Veronica flickered her eyes toward Lucas. "You know that. You knew the truest form of Cathryn, didn't you? In Cape May that summer."

"I knew some of her," he muttered. "What she chose to

share with me. I don't know that it was her truest form, but she was different than she is now."

"That's accurate. The year before you met her, she'd had a crush on a boy she'd met in college. He was deeply in love with someone else. They weren't meant to be, those two, not any more than you and Cathryn were. But still, she was nursing a bruised heart, and I was staying close. I saw what happened with the Senator's case. I was nearby when Tasmyn Vaughn confronted the real murderer. And as I stood there, listening, I was paralyzed, because I knew that voice. I knew that evil. It was the same entity that those men, led by Donald Parcy, had ushered into our world so long before."

"Tasmyn. I know that name." I frowned, looking at Lucas. "Who is she?"

His lip twitched. "Rafe's old . . . flame, I guess. They went to high school together in King. She worked for Carruthers when she was in college."

I remembered now. "And the guy Cathryn had a crush on . . . he was in love with Tasmyn."

Veronica pushed her tea cup away. "Exactly. Oh, it's all so complicated and complex, isn't it? Cathryn fancied herself in love with Michael, who only had eyes for Tasmyn. And then she fell for Lucas, who was meant for you, Jackie. Meanwhile, Rafe thought that Tasmyn was the only girl for him, until he met Nell, who'd tried to kill Tasmyn when they were all still in high school."

I held my head. "It sounds like a soap opera."

"Life is messy, darling." Veronica smiled a little. "Do you think you might warm up my tea before we finish?"

I stood up and added water to the kettle before I put it back on the burner. "So you heard this evil . . . and you realized it was still around."

"Yes. And I was very distressed, because not only was it still in existence, on this plane, but it was very near my family. I began to investigate and research and explore. And what I found was chilling."

We all fell silent as the kettle sang out. I added leaves to Veronica's strainer and poured water slowly over it. Lucas pushed his cup forward, too, for a refill. I thought as I served them how bizarre it was that I was making tea for two vampires. Well, one full-fledged vamp and a half death broker.

"Oh, Jackie. You know, I do enjoy you." Veronica sipped her tea and patted my arm. "But I know what you mean about bizarre. Sometimes I think of Hamlet on that wall in Denmark . . . *There are more things in heaven and earth, Horatio, than are dreamt of in your philosophy.*"

"Exactly!" I returned the kettle to the stove and sat down again. "I have a game I play with Rafe, where I think up different creatures and ask him if they're real or not."

She spread her hands on the table. "Here I was a vampire for centuries, yet I had no inkling what demons were, how they existed or what they might do. I've learned more following Carruthers and their investigations than I did for hundreds of years before."

"Are there such things as vampire slayers?" I inquired. "Oh, and have you ever met vampires like Angel or Spike? Because if I were a vampire and I knew them, I'd be all over that. I'd be hitting that hard."

Lucas gave a discreet cough. "Um, hello, Jacks. Right here. Your half-vampire boyfriend, remember?"

I rolled my eyes. "You're new to the game, and you're more like what Giles might be like if he were vamped." I leaned over and kissed his cheek. "But don't worry. Giles is hot, too."

Veronica smiled. "I haven't met anyone who is a dedicated vampire slayer, no. As far as I know, Buffy is a purely fictional product of Joss Whedon's incredible imagination." She tilted her head, considering. "But I like to think that if she did exist, we'd be friends. We're more alike than different, and after all, I wouldn't be trying to eat her friends."

"But back to the topic at hand." Lucas glared at me. "So you realized the evil that had been set free in 1967 was still around. What came next?"

"As I said, I began researching everything. I followed some hunches, and I spoke to some people I'd met over the years. Certain things that I'd always dismissed as lunacy or fancy, I began to take seriously. And after years—centuries—of working hard to block thoughts from my head, I began to listen. I found that I could trace that evil.

"I wasn't always successful in following its path. From what I've been able to discern, in the beginning, the demon possessed one body at a time for long stretches, staying under the radar as it learned more about our world. But more recently, and certainly since Tasmyn dealt it a slight blow, it's jumped around a bit. It had lived within a man named Ben Ryan for quite a while, but since that time, it seemed to go from body to body."

"Is the demon in Mallory Jones?" I knew that Mallory was a powerful witch, someone who had committed murder more than once. She had killed Joss, Rafe's girlfriend before he'd known Nell, when Joss and Rafe had been working undercover on one of the Hive's communes.

Veronica shook her head. "It doesn't seem likely. Mallory coexisted along with Ben Ryan at times, both of them performing horrible deeds. I think Mallory's form of evil is within her. I don't think it originates from an outside source."

"All right. We've gotten as far as you following the demon to Ben Ryan and then here and there afterward. What happened next?" Lucas shifted, his expression grim. We were getting closer to his first encounter with Veronica, and I could tell that it was making him tense.

"Rafe and Joss went undercover, and Joss was killed. I should have been there, but at that point, I was on the West Coast, trying to get through to Donald Parcy and the other four leaders who'd let the demon over. By the time I realized what was happening, I was too late." She looked inexorably sad. I wished I could offer some kind of reassurance.

"I didn't realize Rafe was still alive in the camp, so instead of going after him, I followed Cathryn to Cape May. I was worried about her. Being near her, I could feel her pain. Her guilt. She was being consumed by remorse for something she could never have foreseen, given her limited understanding of the wider circumstances at the time. So when she met you . . ." Veronica smiled at Lucas. "I was glad. You were good for her, dear one. You kept her from self-destructing, when I think she was on a dangerous brink. In another situation, you two would have been perfect together. Cathryn needs someone strong in her life, because she herself is such a strong person. But she also needs a man who sees how beautiful her soul is and understands that her chilly exterior hides a very tender heart."

I tried hard not to snort. I'd known Cathryn Whitmore for a little while now, and while I was all on board with the chilly exterior, I'd yet to see evidence of the tender heart.

"However, even though I wished I could give you both

my blessing, I knew that it was not meant to be. I'd been in touch with a prognosticator and—what you call a precognitive—and she had foretold *you*, Jackie. She also told me about the man who is meant for Cathryn. While in the short term, I realize that what happened between the two of you was painful, Lucas, I think you know the truth now. Jackie is your destiny. She's the one you need, and she's also going to be an important part of our fight against the Hive."

Lucas reached for my hand and linked our fingers. He pressed a kiss to my cheek. "There's no doubt in my mind that Jackie is my future. I would die for her, and I plan to live with her for the rest of our days, however long or short that time is. But I'll be honest. The idea that we were manipulated by someone . . . it doesn't sit well."

"You weren't manipulated, Lucas." Veronica turned her cup in one slow circle. "I didn't force Cathryn's hand. That night in Cape May, when you'd gone out and Cathryn sat alone in her room at the Star on the Sea, I let her hear my thoughts. I wanted her to be prepared. But I didn't threaten her, and I didn't warn her specifically. The choice was hers. And she made it herself."

"But what about my choice, Veronica? You made that for me, didn't you? I don't remember you asking me if I wanted to be turned. I didn't even have as much of a say in my future as you did when Diego changed you."

"Of course you're right, Lucas." Veronica spoke softly. "My only excuse is that when I realized what had to be done, time was of the essence. My prognosticator friend, when she told me about you and Jackie, had explained that you were destined to be a death broker. You were going to be a key player in the upcoming battle. But she said it was unclear as to which side you would join. Shortly before I spoke with her, I had made a disturbing discovery. Diego had joined with the forces of the Hive. He's working with them. I feared that he might try to recruit you for their purposes.

"I had seen enough of you in Cape May that I had faith you'd choose the light, not the dark, and I knew that giving you the gift of vampirism would make you more powerful. It would give you—all of us—an advantage against the dark."

Lucas didn't drop his gaze from Veronica's face. "All good reasons. But you never offered them to me."

"I did not. You wouldn't have believed me if I had tried to tell you. And . . . the change had to be that night. It had to be simultaneous with your evolution to death broker or it wouldn't work. You wouldn't have changed after the evolution was complete. I didn't have any choice."

"So you seduced me."

I knew this, in theory. Lucas had told me the story early in our relationship. At the time, it hadn't mattered; neither of us were children, and we both had history. But now, faced with this exquisite woman across from me, someone who would always have something in common with Lucas, a bond that he and I would never share, a spark of jealousy zinged through me.

"I didn't know any other way. I was honest when I told you that I've never changed anyone else. Catching your eye in the bar, plying you with alcohol . . . all of it was the only way I knew."

When Lucas didn't respond, Veronica added, "Think about this rationally, dear one. If I had come to you and told you all of this the day we met, what would you have said?"

He lifted one shoulder. "Probably, I would've thought you

were whack job. But I guess we'll never know, will we?"

"Veronica." I had a question, too. "Why did you come to us now? Lucas and Cathryn have been searching for you ever since he came down to Florida. Why tonight?"

She regarded me with fond compassion. "You already know the answer to that question, Jackie. Or at least you know part of the answer, even if it's one you wish were not so. I'm here tonight because the time is coming when we must all join together to fight the darkness, once and for all. You and Lucas will leave your friends here and prepare for the war."

I nodded. "That's the part I know. What about the part I don't?"

Her mouth twisted. "When I began to watch over my family from afar, all those years ago, I made myself a promise. I would never interfere with their lives, not unless it was in the direst of circumstances. I knew, for instance, that I could never watch any of my descendants go hungry if I could feed them. Nor would I ever stand by and let them commit any horrendous act. But otherwise, I was determined to remain only a spectator. To do otherwise was unfair.

"I kept that promise until I realized the demon was still active and in direct opposition to the mission of Carruthers. And even then, I stayed in the background. But now I'm going to have to go against what I felt was the right thing to do all these years. I'm going to interact with them, speak with them . . . and I suppose before I did that, I wanted an ally. I wanted to explain myself." She spread her long fingers on the table and stared down at them. "When I look at Cathryn and at her mother Diana, I don't see two virtual strangers. I see bits of my Benito and Adriano. I see some of my granddaughters, whom I watched grow up from babyhood to be old women. I see my own mother and father, and my sisters and brothers, all long dead now and forgotten by everyone but me." She gazed at us imploringly. "For centuries, I've been alone. Now that I'm about to change that, I'm terrified. All I ask is that you tell Cathryn what I've done. I want to help defeat the Hive.

"I want to help you save the world."

Chapter 8

"THESE CUBES ARE too big."

I lifted my eyes from the cutting board in front of me to see what Charlie held in her hand. She'd scooped up some of the potatoes I'd just finished chopping and was now giving me what I'd privately begun to call her stare of death.

"They're fine." I wasn't in the mood to play culinary wars. We had a limited amount of time in the diner's kitchen; I didn't like to try to work around the regular cooks who served our customers, so I'd decided that Charlie and I would work after hours as much as we could. Tonight's goal was prepping the two potato dishes, as we could easily re-heat them on the morning of the brunch. Earlier in the week, we'd made the sausage patties. The French toast and bacon had to be done on the day of the event, and the omelets would be made to order.

I hadn't co-cooked with anyone professionally since the last summer I'd worked at my dad's restaurant in upstate New York. And even then, my partners had been people I'd known all of my life, including my brothers. We'd had a rhythm, and since most of us had been trained by the same person—my dad—we kept that rhythm easily. We flowed like a river.

But things weren't quite the same with Charlie. As quiet as she was most of the time, in the kitchen, she was bossy and dominating. She was as sure of her ability to cook as she seemed insecure about the rest of her life. And she certainly never hesitated to tell me when I was doing something wrong.

"They're *not* fine." She jiggled her hand so that the small squares of red potato tumbled against each other like dice. "If the potato cubes aren't uniform, they won't cook evenly. Some will be raw and others will be burnt."

"I'm sorry. I don't have a ruler for measuring fucking potato squares." I dropped the knife on the counter and glared at Charlie. "This isn't the food Olympics. We're not cooking for the president or the Queen of England. They're a bunch of old people who won't be happy unless they have something to complain about. By offering them a variety of potato sizes, we're giving them that chance. Look at it as a bonus."

If I'd expected Charlie to back down, I'd have been disappointed. "It doesn't matter who we're cooking for or how important you think the meal is. Every time, we should be giving it our best. Otherwise, what's the point in doing it at all?"

I turned my back to her and held tightly to the edge of the counter, my fingers turning white while mentally I counted to ten. I liked Charlie. At least in theory, I did. When I lay in bed at night, reviewing my day, I was usually grateful that she was part of it. Maybe not during the time I was actually interacting with her, but afterward, sure. The during part drove me crazy sometimes.

I knew that some of my anxiety had nothing to do with Charlie. In the days since Veronica's visit, I'd been walking on eggshells, waiting for the something to happen. After she'd left that night—well, technically it has been the following morning by the time she'd disappeared down my front walk—I'd texted Nell that we were fine and would call in the morning. I should've known better, because within moments of me hitting *send*, Lucas's phone was ringing.

He'd talked to Cathryn for at least forty-five minutes, trying to condense her many-times-over great grandmother's story into a reassuring sound bite. In the end, Cathryn had decided that she would plan a trip down to see us, since there was no way I could make a trip up to Carruthers at the moment, and Lucas didn't feel comfortable leaving Mrs. Mac and me.

Which brought me to the second reason for my constant state of anxiety. There hadn't been any more suspicious deaths since Rachael Hilton had died, but I was still worried about Mrs. Mac. She'd had a couple of weird phone calls—just hang-ups, but still. We were all on edge, and anything out of the ordinary made us even jumpier. Charlie had begun sleeping at her house every night; it was her own idea, which did help to endear her to me. A little bit, anyway.

I had even called Nell to ask if there were any kind of protection spell we could extend from Mrs. Mac's home all the way to the other side of Lucas's property. But she'd told me regretfully that none of her spells worked to ward against humans; they would only ensure that we were alerted to the presence of supernatural evil, not the same kind that lurked in the heart of man . . . or woman.

The police hadn't been much help, either. They'd figured out that whoever was murdering these women had been wearing gloves, and they believed the perpetrator was a male, judging from the size of the finger marks. Still, they couldn't be certain. Some women, I'd noticed, had rather large hands. I found myself surreptitiously checking the hand sizes of the Ms. Florida Senior Living Pageant contestants, just in case.

All of the surviving contestants had been warned to be on alert and not to allow strangers into their homes. Privately, I felt that was useless advice, since it seemed the murder victims had allowed the killer into their houses. But it didn't hurt to make everyone aware. Although we were worried about Mrs. Mac, there was no evidence that she was in any more danger than the rest of the would-be beauty queens, despite her loud proclamations that she was the next most likely winner and thus had her head on the chopping block.

I was just about to tackle my next potato when I felt Charlie come up behind me. She reached around and took away the colander of potatoes, replacing it with a bowl of red, green and orange peppers.

"You work on the peppers, and I'll finish the potatoes. Makes more sense, anyway. And when you're finished with the peppers, you could start grating the potatoes for the hash browns."

"Are you sure I'm capable of handling that job?" I heard the resentful bite to my own words.

But Charlie could take it as well as she dished, and she only shrugged. "Size doesn't matter when it comes to shredded potatoes. They're just going to get mixed up in the batter, shaped and fried."

I couldn't think of anything to reply to that, so I shut my mouth and began slicing and dicing the peppers.

It was odd, I mused as I chopped that some people came into my life unexpectedly and immediately took up an important role. That hadn't been the case in my first thirty years or so, when my family and childhood friends had dominated the landscape of my days. Even with Will, my erstwhile fiancé who, it had turned out, had been married with kids all the while he was planning a future with me, it hadn't been love at first sight. He'd wooed me, taking months before we even had our first date. That had made his ultimate betrayal even more painful. I'd been careful and cautious and looked before I leapt. And what had it gotten me? A houseful of wedding gifts I had to return and an endless supply of sympathetic, pitying looks from people who'd heard that poor Jackie had been duped.

Maybe that was why, when I'd met Lucas, I hadn't been so hesitant. After all, if being careful hadn't helped me suss out a loser before, why bother? And as it had turned out, Lucas was the most honorable, upright man I'd ever known outside my dad and my brothers. Even taking into account his death broker/half vamp status, he still took better care of my heart than anyone I'd ever dated. I hadn't needed to hear Veronica's words about the two of us being fated for a lifetime together to know that was true.

Opening the door to Lucas, though, had meant a whole passel of new friends. Nichelle, Rafe, Nell . . . even Cathryn, though I still wasn't sure either of us would term each other friends. And then I'd met Crissy Darwin, who still messaged us regularly from the road and from Nashville, where she'd gone to launch the next phase of her recording career. Now,

Charlie had joined the mix. I wasn't sure if she complicated things or would, in the end, make our lives easier, but she seemed to be here to stay.

We hadn't talked about Reg's bar since the day we'd gone over there to pack up dishes. Neither Lucas nor I wanted to push her. He had, however, gently inquired as to whether or not she wanted to have some kind of service to send Reg off into the next life.

Charlie had deferred, saying Reg wasn't religious and wouldn't want a fuss. She pointed out that even if we had a funeral of sorts, it was entirely possible that the three of us would be the only ones in attendance. I'd begun to argue that having owned a bar for years, his patrons would likely take part, but Lucas had shot me a warning glance and a slight shake of his head. We'd dropped the subject.

I glanced over my shoulder and watched her knife fly through the potatoes, creating evenly-sized cubes. She clearly had both talent and passion when it came to cooking.

"Why did you go to culinary school?"

If my breaking the silence between us surprised her, Charlie didn't react. Her fingers never missed a beat. I half-expected her to shrug and give me a one-syllable answer. But instead, I heard her inhale a deep breath.

"It was mostly because of Reg. Not that he pushed me or thought it was a good idea, but he's the one who taught me the basics of cooking. When Aunt Val and I moved in with him . . . well, I loved Aunt Val. She was cool, and she took good care of me. She worked hard, and for a long time, we had that 'you and me against the world' thing going for us. But a cook she was not. Her idea of meal planning was to go through the aisles at the grocery store and dump as much frozen crap into her basket as possible. Sometimes she'd tried to see how long we could go without shopping—she hated it—so she'd stock up the freezer and buy shit like powdered milk." Charlie shuddered.

I laughed. "She was probably from the generation that believed the more you could do with packaged food and the microwave, the better. I had friends up in New York when I was a kid whose parents were like that. They used to be so jealous of the homemade meals my dad cooked. We didn't even own a microwave for a long time."

"Aunt Val didn't always know how to work the stove, but yeah, the microwave was her best friend. It just wasn't important to her, you know? Meals were something we had to do to stay alive, but they didn't have to be important. We never owned a table until after she met Reg."

"Ah. Things changed at that point?" I finished another pepper and reached for a new one.

"Oh, yeah. The first time I met him, he cooked for us. He made us fried chicken, mashed potatoes and collard greens. I remember Aunt Val told him I'd never eat all that—the closest thing I'd had up to that point was out of a frozen dinner tray, and we never had anything green on our plates—but I loved it. And Reg loved watching me eat.

"After that, I wanted to learn how he did it. I guess part of me figured it was only a matter of time before he dumped Val or she dumped him, so I'd better get all the education I could while Reg still liked us. So he taught me the basics." In one swift and efficient move, Charlie scooped the cubed potatoes from the cutting board into the large bowl at her side.

"What did your Aunt Val think of that?" I imagined she might have been a little defensive about this guy she'd just met offering her niece a different perspective on cooking. And eating.

"At first, she was just surprised. She told me later that she'd never had any clue I wanted more when it came to our kinds of meals. She and my mom had been raised the same way she was bringing me up, so she didn't know any different. Once she said to me that she always figured home-cooked meals and families eating around a table were things that only happened in television shows. Like, it was some kind of fairy tale."

I bit the edge of my lip. "That's kind of sad."

"Yeah, it was. Once she understood that I wasn't really being critical of her ways—I just wanted to make our lives better—she was fine with Reg teaching me. And pretty soon, it was clear the two of them had it bad for each other, so I began to relax and trust that we were really going to stick together, you know? We moved in with him over the bar, and that was the best thing ever. I had access to a kitchen all the time, and Reg and I used to watch cooking shows together. Some of it we'd laugh at, but a lot of the recipes we actually did try ourselves."

"What did Reg like to cook? When I think of a bar, I think mostly fried stuff and burgers."

Charlie nodded. "Yeah, you'd be right. Reg . . . well, if you ever saw him, you'd understand that he wasn't vegetarian. He didn't eat clean. He told me that there was too much good food in the world to ever consider the word *diet*. So sometimes we'd make onion rings at midnight, or we'd have mozzarella sticks as our main course. Reg was a great cook, but he wasn't much of a nutritionist."

I remembered Lucas telling me that Reg's fatal heart attack had come on the heels of a breakfast that included cheese fries. I decided Charlie was being generous in her description.

"Anyway, though, after Aunt Val got cancer, I started researching different ways food could affect things like healing and disease. But I was just a kid, and she was pretty far along before she was diagnosed. She wouldn't even try to change how she ate. Even after she died, Reg wasn't very interested in what I was learning about food and health—we were both pretty depressed in those days. We cooked together more than we talked."

"It can be healing. Cooking together." I dumped the last bit of diced peppers into my bowl and reached for a bag of potatoes to begin peeling before I grated them. "After my nana died, my friend Al—he owned this diner, and he was my dear friend. I still miss him. One of the ways he got me out of the house and helped me begin to move on was by asking me to cook with him, right here in this kitchen."

"Yeah, exactly." Charlie passed me the large grater without me even asking for it. "By the time I was in my senior year of high school, I'd taken over making most of our meals. Reg cooked in the bar, but I handled all the food upstairs. One night, I was telling him about this guidance counselor at school who was trying to get me to decide what I was going to do after graduation. I had decent grades, and I worked hard, but I knew the money wasn't there for college. So we had this cooking show on TV—it was an old Julia Child, actually—and Reg poked me in the arm and said, 'That's what you should do. Go to school for cooking.'"

"That was the first time you'd considered it?"

She shrugged. "I guess. Cooking was fun, you know? It wasn't anything I thought I could make into a career. But when Reg said that, I started looking into what was around, and it turned out one of the most highly-rated culinary schools is connected with our community college system. I qualified for a full-ride, and so . . ." She tossed me a half-smile over her shoulder. "I got to go to college *and* to culinary school."

"What did you plan to do after graduation? You said you'd just finished a little while before Reg . . . passed."

"I was going to keep helping him at the bar. I'd had some vague ideas about maybe adding a restaurant there, but I wasn't sure about that, and neither was he. At school, they put the fear of God into us about how cutthroat this business can be. A bunch of people who graduated with me went down and got jobs at the resorts, and they all work pretty much non-stop." She finished her last potato and reached for some onions. "I don't mind working hard, but I don't want to be used, and I like having control over my hours. I don't want to be screamed at, either. Not when I know I'm doing my best."

"Hmmm." I thought of my father's restaurant up in New York. My dad had often taken on new culinary school graduates as interns, letting them train under him. I realized how lucky those baby chefs had been; that kitchen was always a nurturing environment, as my father had the biggest, softest heart around. Charlie would have loved working with him.

The ringing of a bell over the door interrupted my thoughts. I must've forgotten to lock it; if it were Lucas coming in now, I was about to face a scolding. He was on top of all of us to be more aware and more careful in the wake of the local murders.

But it wasn't his face that peered through the swinging kitchen door. Instead, Nichelle grinned at me.

"Hey, ladies. I stopped by your place with a delivery, and Lucas told me where you were. Need a hand?" Nichelle was a passionate amateur chef; it had been her appreciation for my work as a food columnist that had cemented our friendship initially.

I glanced at Charlie, but she only shook her head. "Once you finished grating those, most of the scut work is done. I'll start frying up the potatoes. Other than mixing up the hash browns, we're done here tonight, if you want to take a break."

Nichelle raised one eyebrow at me. "I seem to recall that we left a bottle of red wine here the last time I came by. Think it's still hidden in the pantry?"

Laughing, I rinsed off my hands and dried them on a towel. "Probably. We hid it pretty well. Go on out and find us a table, and I'll bring out the bottle and some glasses."

After the door had swished closed again, I turned to Charlie. "Are you sure about this? I don't want to dump all the work on you."

"Yeah, it's good. If you don't mind handling the hash browns . . ." She frowned, her eyebrows knitting together, and then her eyes lit up. "I just had an idea. I read about it somewhere a few weeks back—we don't have to deep fry the hash browns. We can use a waffle iron."

I cocked my head. "A waffle iron? That's—" I thought about it for a moment. "That's brilliant. We have a Belgian waffle iron here. Using that would let us essentially make four hash browns at a time. And those we could do ahead of time, too."

"A lot less mess than using the deep fryer, too." Charlie gave one brief, decisive nod. "I'll start pouring those while I do the home fries on the stove top. Go ahead out with Nichelle. I've got this."

Leaving the kitchen in the middle of a job gave me a

strange feeling, but I hadn't had a real visit with Nichelle in a while. So I found our bottle of wine, snagged two goblets from the case of glassware and went to join my friend.

She was ensconced in a booth, scrolling through her phone. "Bring that right over here, girlfriend. I've had a long day, and I earned this break."

Chuckling, I poured each of us a glass and sat down across from her. "*Slainte mhaith.*" Out of habit, I used the Irish toast my grandmother had favored before I touched my goblet to Nichelle's.

"Yeah, cheers." Nichelle gave me a crooked grin and took a sip. "So how's it going in there with girl wonder?"

"Actually, if you'd gotten here about thirty minutes earlier, you'd have thought I was going to wring her neck. She was criticizing my potato chopping technique."

Nichelle's eyes went wide as she clapped a hand to her heart. "The nerve! And yet she still breathes?"

"Yeah. Charlie doesn't pull any punches, and tact isn't quite her thing, but she's a damn good chef. I'm lucky to have her working with me." I realized it was true even as I said it.

"Is this going to be a permanent thing, then?" Nichelle quirked one eyebrow my way.

I shrugged. "I don't know. Maybe." I traced one finger in a circle around the base of my wine glass. "Lucas thinks it would be a good idea for me to have someone who could cover for me, in case we have to be . . . out of the loop for a while."

"Ah." She was silent for a few minutes. "You okay, Jackie? Anything you need to tell me?"

I drew in a deep breath. "I really can't. Not yet." *Maybe not ever.* Trying to explain to my friend why I would be leaving town wasn't going to be easy.

"Are you sick? Or are you pregnant?" She leaned forward, her face intense.

"What?" I frowned. "No. Neither. What would make you think that?"

She tilted her head. "Oh, I don't know. You've been acting a little weird lately, like there's something you want to tell me but can't. And then Charlie appears and moves in with you, and suddenly you're talking about being out of the loop. In my experience, that means you're either thinking about treatments or maternity leave."

"I guess I can see that. But no, I'm neither knocked up nor sick. Thank God." Out of instinct and habit, I crossed myself, and Nichelle did the same.

"Then where do you think you're going? Why would you be unavailable and need someone like Charlie?"

The answers I had weren't going to make any sense to Nichelle, but I also knew I couldn't placate her with non-information. We'd never lied to each other before, even if I hadn't always been forthcoming who and what Lucas was. That topic was an area where by mutual, tacit agreement, we both avoided saying or asking anything that might force me into having to lie.

I stalled a little, topping off our wine. "Nichelle . . . if something were to happen, do you have a safe place to go? You and George and the kids?"

She sat back, studying me. "Define safe. Are we talking, like, weather? A tornado shelter? Or terrorism? Level with me, Jackie. What are you and Lucas involved in?"

"I wish I could tell you everything, but it would put you in danger. More danger. Even if I did tell you, you wouldn't believe me."

"Try me." She folded her arms over her chest, leaning them on the table.

"God, Nichelle. Please. Just trust me on this one, you don't want to know."

"Jackie, I deliver bags of blood to your boyfriend every three days. He's not a medical professional, and as far as I can see, he's not sick. It's not my job to ask what he does with that blood, but I have thoughts. Hunches. In my line of work, I deal with a lot of weird-ass shit, and I try not to think about it. I'd never ask you to betray a confidence, but right now, you're bringing me something. And you're saying things that make me think you're trying to warn me. I need more. I need to know what I might be dealing with."

I nodded. "Okay. That's fair." I wracked my brain, trying to think of the best way to frame a serious warning without making Nichelle feel like she had to report me to the authorities as a mental case. "There's the potential of something serious going down in the near future. It won't be like anything you've ever experienced, although at first, I guess you might think it's nothing more than another terrorist attack or political unrest. Honestly, I'm not really sure what might happen in the beginning. But if things go south, you need to have a plan. That's what I want you to understand."

"What about you and Lucas? Where will you be?"

I forced a smile. "I'm not sure, but it won't be around here. We're going to do everything in our power to make sure things don't get to the point where you'd be in danger. We want to stop the danger before it reaches the rest of the world. But in order to do that, we're going to have to go away for a little while, I think. Unless something changes dramatically in the next month or so, Lucas and I have to leave. With any luck, we'll be back and you won't even understand what really happened. I can't leave town, though, without knowing you all are as prepared as you can be."

She stared at me for several minutes. "Okay. Tell me what we need to do."

I hadn't gotten very far along the way in this process. "When—if—the world starts to spin out of control, you're going to need more than shelter and physical safety. You're going to need to be protected from evil." I hesitated. "The church. In an emergency, could you go to a church?"

"Sure. We could go to St. Crispin's." Her face darkened. "So that's what we're talking about, huh? Spiritual warfare kind of stuff?"

I reached across the table to lay a hand on her arm. "There's evil in the world, Nichelle, and it has the potential to be serious. Like . . . world-ending serious. If I'm not around to help, I need to know you're going to be okay. Or at least that you'll have a plan." I worried my lip between my teeth. "And I also want to ask you for a favor. I won't be here to keep my eye on Mrs. Mac. If things get dicey, would you watch out for her?"

"You know I will." She nodded. "What about Charlie?"

"Yeah, that was going to be my next question. Lucas and I are hoping she'll stick around to oversee the diner and our houses while we're away, and so she'll be there for Mrs. Mac on a daily basis and to take care of Makani. It's only in case of an emergency that I'd need you to jump in as backup."

"Of course. I love Mrs. Mac and Makani, and Charlie . . . well, we'll rub along. Don't worry about us. I'll cover you here."

"Thanks, Nichelle. I appreciate that. I don't know what's going to happen, but I feel better with you in charge around here. I'm hoping that I still have a life to come back to afterward."

"Are you sure there isn't anything else I can do?" Nichelle smirked. "I'm not a bad chick to have on your side in a fight. Just saying."

"Hey, if you didn't have little kids, I'd be recruiting you. I have no doubts of your mad skills. But George and the children need you. So it's better that you keep the home front safe for now." I paused. "Hey, Nichelle. As long as we're asking and answering questions, how did you get involved in this business? I mean, I get the feeling there's a story there."

She smiled at me, her eyes glittering. "Oh, there is. But it's not one for tonight. Tell you what—when all of this is over, you and I will sit down with a bottle of scotch and we'll tell all our stories. You can spill the truth on Lucas, and I'll come clean on my career."

"It's a date." I raised my wine glass and tapped it against Nichelle's again. "Save the world, drink some scotch."

"If that's not an incentive for getting the job done, I don't know what is." Nichelle slid out of the booth and stood up, stretching. "Now let's go invade Charlie's kitchen and make her have a glass of wine, too. I'm bound and determined to see that girl unwind a little before the world goes up in a ball of flames."

Chapter 9

"JACKIE, CAN YOU bring out another tray of home fries?" Charlie poked her head into the kitchen of the Golden Rays Community Center. "They're going fast. I hope we made enough."

"It'll be fine." I bent over the oven and lifted out the aluminum pan. "If we run short, we'll just push the hash browns."

"True." She was flushed, and with her short hair tucked behind her ears, she looked about fourteen years old. "They all seem to like the food, though."

"Of course they do. We made an incredible brunch. Here're the home fries. Now, do you need me to take over the omelet station for a little while?"

"No, I'm good." She took the pan from me and back through the door. "I'll let you know if we need anything else."

I spent some time chopping a few more omelet ingredients

to send out to Charlie, just in case, checked on the rest of food and put on a new pot of coffee. The noise level in the dining room swelled, and I peeked out the door to see what was going on.

The line for food was still moving, but across the room, I saw a line of women sashaying through the door. A splattering of applause spread over the crowd, and someone called out, "Welcome to our Ms. Florida Senior Living Pageant contestants!"

Mrs. Mac brought up the rear. She walked with a deliberate grace, glancing left and right, putting into practice the royal wave she'd been rehearsing for the last week. Her gray hair was piled high on her head, and she wore a long dress of glittering silver that seemed particularly incongruous with the morning light shining in through the windows. Nichelle had helped with her makeup, and from this distance, I had to admit that she looked at least five years younger.

The contestants made their way to the reserved table at the front of the room. A couple of the organizers and other volunteers approached the buffet line and began filling plates so that the ladies didn't have to move from their seats to enjoy the food. I grinned, shaking my head.

"Well, we got them here, all safe and accounted for." Behind me, Lucas slid an arm around my waist and looked over my shoulder, following my gaze. "No murders in a week."

"I don't know how much *we* had to do with it," I said wryly. "We kept our eye on Mrs. Mac, but that didn't do anything for the remaining eleven ladies. I think it was just luck . . . or else the other murders were coincidence."

"What about Mrs. Mac's phone calls?" He arched a brow at me.

"Who knows? Maybe it was just circumstantial. At any rate, the whole thing seems to be over now. The only worry we have is what to do when Mrs. Mac doesn't win the crown. We're going to have to be there to make her feel better. Help her drown her sorrows."

"What makes you think she won't win?" Lucas's lips tipped up into a half-smile. "She's got as much chance as the others, right?"

"In theory, yes. But you haven't heard her sing. And once the judges do, I'm afraid it's going to mean the end of her pageant dreams, once and for all."

"Okay. I see what you mean."

Next to me, Lucas slumped down in his folding chair, his face a study in pain. "I didn't think . . . was that the love song from *South Pacific* or the mating call of a wildebeest? Good God."

On my other side, Nichelle sighed. "On the plus side, she looked damned gorgeous while she was, uh, warbling."

"That's true." I leaned over to see Charlie. "How did she seem when you left her right before she went on stage? You were the last one to see her."

"She was typical Mrs. Mac. You know, confident and positive she's going to win. She was only worried that the women who haven't performed their talent yet were going to be so disheartened that they wouldn't go on."

I glanced up at the stage, where a rather large lady was

preparing to play the harp. "That doesn't seem to be an issue."

"She's going to lose, isn't she?" Lucas sighed. "You were right. We better stock up on cheap wine and chocolate."

"I think I'll sneak backstage and check on her." I stood up and hunched over so as not to block the view of those sitting behind us. "She really did have her heart set on winning this. I want to make sure she's able to lose gracefully and not stage a coup."

Lucas grimaced. "Good luck with that."

I groped my way through the darkened rows of chairs that made up the make-shift theater in the community center's all-purpose room. In spite of Mrs. Mac's claims otherwise, this pageant was run on a shoestring budget. The brunch had been cleared away, tables folded and chairs reconfigured before the curtain went up on the small stage at the far end of the room. The pageant officials had even sweet-talked me into agreeing to cater the brunch at cost. I hadn't been happy about it, but out of respect for Mrs. Mac and Charlie, I'd said yes.

The backstage area was actually a glorified hallway. Most of the contestants were seated in the front row of the audience to support their fellow performers, but I hadn't seen Mrs. Mac emerge to take her own seat there. I was afraid that she was sulking back here, too mortified to show her face after the debacle of her song.

There weren't any windows in that hall, and the light was very dim. I slipped in through the door, scanning the narrow room to find my friend. A rolling closet along the wall was stuffed with dresses, and the rest of the floor was littered with boxes and various props. I spotted the guitar that one would-be queen had played before Mrs. Mac's turn next to a music stand with papers scattered on it.

But I didn't see Mrs. Mac. I was just about to turn around go back to my seat, assuming that I'd missed her back in the audience, when a sound caught my attention. Frowning, I looked toward the far corner on the other side of the closet, where one of the shadows . . . moved.

"Mrs. Mac? Is that you, honey? C'mon, don't hide back here." I walked over slowly, giving her a few seconds to compose herself. "It wasn't . . . well, it wasn't as bad as you're thinking. Please don't be upset."

As my vision adjusted to the lack of light, I realized that there were actually two figures in the corner. One was taller and clothed in a long black gown and some kind of cape with a hood that obscured her face. I thought, as I stepped closer, that she was comforting Mrs. Mac, whom I could recognize thanks to the silver sequins of her gown.

But then I got a better look at the situation and saw to my horror that the taller woman had her gloved hands around Mrs. Mac's throat. Mrs. Mac was trying to pull away the attacker's fingers, but her swats were ineffectual, and her eyes were rolling back into her head.

With a cry that was half-yelp, half-scream, I threw myself at both of them. The woman trying to kill Mrs. Mac was solid, and I staggered backward a little before I launched my second assault.

"Get *away*!" It was not a woman's voice that growled at me. "I'll take care of you in a minute. I don't have time for any more stubborn meddling bitches. I'm going to have this contract, and I'm going to drive all of you out, one way or the other."

She—he?—shook me loose and turned his attention back to Mrs. Mac, who'd begun to sag alarmingly. I screamed once more and tackled him, clawing for the cape, for his hands—anything to buy us some time.

"Get the hell *off*!" Suddenly and out of nowhere, Charlie was next to me, her arms around the killer's neck, her legs hooked at his waist in a bizarre imitation of a piggy back. Smart girl that she was, her fingers were on his face, covering his eyes and tearing at his skin.

And then Nichelle was alongside me, too, pulling Mrs. Mac toward her, and Lucas shoved the man in the long black dress against the wall before he yanked off the hood and punched him in the mouth with a wicked right hook.

As the hood fell away, I gasped. Augustus Row sagged against the wall, blood pouring from his mouth even as his eyes still blazed.

"Fucking *bitches*." He snarled the words at us, ignoring Lucas who was still pinning him into the wall. "You made me do it. *You* made me do it all. I didn't want to kill anyway. But then those bitches wouldn't play nice. They wouldn't just sign on the dotted line, agree to sell their houses like they should've. No, they had to get stubborn. They wouldn't play ball. But I want that contract. I have to have it. So if they wouldn't go easy, they had to go hard. And I'm not too good to get my hands dirty to take care of business."

Nichelle was on her cell, calling for the police and for the ambulance. Mrs. Mac was on the floor, but to my immense relief, she was sitting up, blinking at us even as she clutched at her throat.

"He wanted my house." Her voice was hoarse, and she coughed, trying to clear it. "I wouldn't let him sell it for me, and so he . . . I was back here after my number, and I thought he was another contestant. One of our bigger boned gals.

Then the next thing I knew, he had me back here and he was squeezing my neck, just squeezing until I couldn't breathe."

Charlie knelt next to Mrs. Mac. "Shhh. It's okay. We took care of the son of a bitch." She glared at Augustus.

"The contract is *mine*." Row struggled to get away from Lucas, hissing the words. "It's my gravy train. He promised me a cut on each house I listed. And I want them all. *All!*"

"I think he's lost it." Lucas shook his head. "Do you know what he's talking about?"

"I'm not sure." I frowned. "He got a lot of people at Golden Rays to list their homes with him. Maybe he was on the take from someone else." I glanced at Augustus, but apparently he'd decided to dummy up about then, because he only narrowed his eyes at me and snapped shut his mouth.

"Oh, my goodness, what happened? What's going on?" The small backstage area was suddenly crowded with the other contestants and the pageant officials, along with some of the audience members. Even the judges were peering in at us.

Before any of us could explain, the police pushed into the room, making way for the paramedics who rolled in a gurney and began examining Mrs. Mac. I heard Nichelle telling a few people what had happened, but she was interrupted by a wail from Mrs. Mac.

"I can't go to the hospital!" She was still husky-voiced, and I could see bruises begin to blossom on her throat. "The pageant isn't over. I'll miss being crowned. I can't do it. Let me stay. I'll go to the hospital after I've heard my name announced and put on my sash."

There were several moments of tense silence. I spotted two of the judges conferring with the head of the pageant, and then to my surprise, several of the contestants joined the whispered conversation.

The EMTs were still trying to convince Mrs. Mac to let them examine her when one of the judges raised her voice, clearing her throat.

"Ahem!" She waved her hand, trying to quiet everyone in the room. "Please. I think I can make this easier." The room fell silent again, and all eyes turned to the judge.

"After conferring with my fellow pageant judges, we've made our decision and we're prepared to announce it a little early. This year Ms. Florida Senior Living Queen is . . ." She paused for dramatic effect, her gaze circling the room.

"Anna MacConnelly!"

For one dizzy moment, I thought to myself, *who is Anna MacConnelly*? And then I understood, as glad relief and gratitude swelled in my heart. Nichelle clapped her hands and whistled, and if I wasn't mistaken, I thought I spied the sheen of tears in Charlie's eyes.

The paramedics helped Mrs. Mac onto the gurney, supporting her on either side as last year's queen approached. She bent over and kissed Mrs. Mac's pale cheek, draped a bright yellow sash over her shoulder and bestowed a small rhinestone tiara onto her head.

Mrs. Mac beamed, waved to her adoring public and allowed the medics to help her lift her feet up onto the stretcher. I knelt beside her and gave her a gentle hug.

"Congratulations, Mrs. Mac! I'm so proud of you."

She smiled at me and patted my cheek. "Well, dear, it was very kind of them to make the announcement as they did."

I squeezed her hand. "Oh, I think they just knew who most deserved the title."

She raised her eyebrows and regarded me in full queen

mode. "Of course they did. After my song, I don't think there could be any question." She lowered her voice and murmured to me, "Frankly, Jackie, I was more surprised they didn't just give me the crown at the end of my performance. But I supposed that they needed to be gracious to the less-talented ladies. I was saying as much to the woman who was backstage with me—well, the one who turned out not to be a woman at all, of course—when she—uh, he—started choking me. I'll be honest; for a minute, I really did think the murderer was a disgruntled contestant who was willing to do anything to win."

"Oh," I managed faintly. "Well, all's well that ends well, right?"

"Very true." She allowed the EMTs to cover her with the sheet and secure her to the gurney. "Watch the crown, please. And can you make sure I'm registered at the hospital as Ms. Florida Senior Living Queen Anna MacConnelly? I don't want anyone to forget who I am."

I swallowed back a sigh. *It was going to be a long year.*

Chapter 10

"NEVER A DULL moment around here, is there?" Charlie poured hot water from the kettle over tea leaves into a cup. "I never knew how boring my life was until I came to live with all of you."

I managed a half-smile. "Yeah, sometimes it feels that way. But I promise, this murder thing isn't a regular occurrence."

"Oh, really?" Charlie narrowed her eyes at me. "Mrs. Mac said you and Lucas were involved in the murders around some local singer. She said you got stabbed."

Wincing, I nodded. "That was . . . just something that happened. And may I point out that this time, it was Mrs. Mac who was the killer's target?"

"True." She set the teacup on a wooden tray and added a small plate of cookies that she'd made earlier in the day. "Still . . ." She fiddled with the napkin on the edge of the saucer. "I wanted to talk to you about something, but then everything got crazy with the pageant and then the attempted murder and Mrs. Mac being in the hospital."

Pulling out a chair, I sat down. "I have a minute now. What's up? Everything okay?"

"I hope so." Charlie sat down, too. "I was thinking about the Stinker. I did some research into what it would take for me to run it, or even what would be involved if I wanted to add a restaurant to the existing business. I have the numbers and the information."

"Is that what you want to do?" I was careful to keep a neutral voice. I didn't want my needs to influence Charlie's final decision.

She shrugged. "I wasn't sure. But the more I think about it, the more I think . . . no. I don't want to be tied down to a business like a bar or a restaurant. I don't want to live upstairs and know that I'm never really getting away from work. I don't want to be tied down to a menu that's determined by what my regulars demand instead of what I want to cook."

"I can understand that." I nodded. "So what is that you *do* want to do?"

She took a deep breath. "I was thinking that maybe I'd sell the bar. Reg owed a little on it, but not as much as I'd thought. I'd make a decent profit. And then I thought maybe . . . I'd invest that money into our business. Our catering business."

Surprise struck me silent. This was really the last thing I'd expected to hear. "*Our* catering business? I didn't know we had one."

"We don't yet. But if you wanted a partner, I'd like to buy in. I'd bring not only talent and hard work, but some capital. I know I'm young, and I know I'm bossy, but I think we could work well together." She finally met my eyes, and in hers, I saw uncertainty, vulnerability and . . . hope. She was reaching out, taking a chance, and I held the power to encourage her or to knock her down again.

Impulsively, I reached over to grab her hand. "Charlie, that's about the most exciting idea I've heard in a long time. I want to talk to Lucas, but I know he'll be all for it, too. And just for your information, even if you didn't bring any money into this deal, I'd still be all for it."

A smile spread over her face. "Cool." She didn't pull her hand away from me, and I counted that as growth. "One more thing. I was wondering if it would be okay for me to move back in with you after Mrs. Mac's better." She hurried to add, "I mean, I love her and all, and she's awesome, but I think she needs her space. She told me the other day that she likes privacy when her, uh, gentlemen friends come over for a visit." Charlie's face went pink.

"Of course you can." I paused. "Actually, I'd like that. There's something we should talk about, as it relates to both business and our living situation." I hoped Charlie would take what I had to say as easily as Nichelle had. "At some point in the not-too-distant future, Lucas and I are probably going to have to go away for a little while. It's related to his, um, other work. I don't know when we'll go, and I don't even know for sure how long we'll be gone. But it would make me feel much better if I knew you were here to take care of our houses and Makani, and to watch out for Mrs. Mac."

Charlie frowned. "Where are you going?"

I shook my head. "I'm sorry. I can't tell you. To be honest, I don't even know at this point. I only know that it's coming."

"Are you guys, like, spies or something? Undercover

agents?"

"Something like that, I guess, but not precisely."

"But you *are* coming back, right? You're not going to just disappear forever?" There was a small thread of panic in Charlie's voice, and my heart almost broke. This girl had been left by her parents of their own free will and by her two surrogate parents when they had died. She was taking a big chance in trusting virtual strangers like Lucas and me. She was opening up to us as well as to Mrs. Mac and Nichelle. The possibility that something might happen that would prevent me from coming home was untenable.

"I have every intention of coming back, Charlie. I promise you. If by some quirk of fate I can't, please know it will not be because I didn't want to return. Count on the fact that if I don't come home, I'm dead."

She snorted. "That's not exactly comforting, Jackie."

I laughed. "Sorry. I tend toward dark humor. But I do mean it. I happen to love my life, Charlie. And that includes all of it—Mrs. Mac, all of our neighbors here . . . and you. Lucas and I will be back, or we'll die trying."

"I'm going to hold you to that." She stood up and lifted the tray. "I'll take this to the Queen, and then I'm going to start a batch of tortilla soup. The chicken broth in it will be good for her throat." Hands full, she nodded toward the window. "Looks like your company is here."

I glanced back over my shoulder to where Rafe and Nell were climbing out of the Impala. Behind them, Cathryn slid from behind the wheel of her powder blue Thunderbird. She looked as impeccable and unflappable as ever, with her white-blonde hair pinned up and her shirt swirling around her knees. But then she hesitated, turning to look behind her, and

I wondered if she was nervous about this meeting.

"That's the ice queen, huh?" Charlie peered out the window. "She's pretty, but she doesn't look like Lucas's type. I wouldn't let her get to you."

I forced a smile, suddenly regretting that I'd spilled my guts to Charlie regarding Lucas and Cathryn's past involvement. I couldn't exactly warn Charlie that Cathryn could hear her thoughts, but I didn't like Cathryn knowing that she still bothered me sometimes.

"Oh, she doesn't get to me," I fibbed. "She's just his boss now. Our boss, that is. And our friend, of course." I decided I'd be better to redirect her attention than to protest too much. "Can I trust you to keep Mrs. Mac company, or are you going to be hanging out the window, drooling over Rafe?"

Charlie sighed. "Mrs. Mac and I will be fine. We might talk about Rafe, and we might drool over him from the safety of this house, but I promise that I won't embarrass you or myself."

"Thanks." With a quick wave, I went outside and headed for Lucas's house, crossing my own yard and climbing the steps to his back deck. My stomach clenched; this was no ordinary meeting. It wasn't a social occasion, certainly. Today, Cathryn was going to meet Veronica for the first time. But even beyond the family reunion, she'd told us over the phone, in her typical cryptic fashion, that she had urgent information for all of us.

Cathryn had tried to convince us to drive up to Carruthers for this meeting, but I wasn't ready to leave Mrs. Mac yet. Lucas had sided with me, and Veronica had also indicated that she preferred to meet Cathryn on neutral ground. Apparently, Lucas's home qualified as such.

"Hey." My boyfriend met me at his door, pulling me into a tight hug. "They're in the living room. Cathryn's so tense, she's practically thrumming, and Veronica isn't here yet. Nell is just sitting there, looking bored, and Rafe is trying to act like everything is normal."

"So . . . same old, same old, huh?" I tiptoed to kiss his cheek. "It'll be fine. Cathryn is too intent on winning this battle to let anything like emotions get in the way. But you have to think that the idea of meeting your ancestor from almost four hundred years ago is a little weird. Add into it the fact that said grandmother is also a vampire, and you've crossed out of weird into downright bizarre."

"Yeah, I get that. We'll get through it." He opened the refrigerator and began pulling out bottles of beer. "But I figured we might get through it better with some alcohol."

"Good idea." I leaned in to take a few from his hands and caught sight of a pile of blood bags sitting on a shelf. "Lucas."

"Hmmm?" He closed the door and turned toward the doorway.

"When did you get a delivery from Nichelle?"

Lucas frowned. "Uh, day before yesterday. She brought me a cooler before we went to the pageant that morning. Why?"

I sucked in my bottom lip. "You usually get three bags. There are like five in there right now."

He closed his eyes and sighed. "Yeah, I know. I had to up my order. I was going through three in a day, and it made me a little anxious that I was going to run out, so I talked to Nichelle and asked her to arrange for more."

"Oh." I'd thought I was accustomed to my boyfriend drinking blood, and usually I was, but the idea that his need was increasing made me uneasy. "Aren't you worried about why you need more? Doesn't that make you wonder why?"

He shifted one bottle of beer to the other hand and opened a drawer to retrieve an opener. "It did, but I talked to Veronica. She said there could be several reasons. One is that I'm beginning to accept the idea that I'm a vampire. Or a half-vamp, whatever you want to call me." He popped off the top of one bottle of beer and then the other. "The other possibility is that I need to build my strength for the coming battle. That may be why I need to drink more from you, too."

My face went hot. I was pretty open with Rafe and Nell about most things, and it was hard to keep a secret from Cathryn, with her ability to hear my thoughts, but I'd never discussed with them what went on between Lucas and me during sex. I wasn't ashamed of the fact that he drank from me when we were intimate, but it was . . . ours. And if I were going to be ashamed of anything, it might be that I actually enjoyed it.

"Did you tell Veronica about that?" I hissed. "About . . . us?"

"Of course not," Lucas returned. "But remember that she can hear things, and remember that she's been observing us for a while. It wouldn't surprise me if she knows already."

There was a soft knock at the door behind us, and Veronica stepped into the kitchen. I tried to compose myself, tried to think of anything but the things I didn't want her to know. But of course, as these things work, suddenly that was all I *could* think about.

"I'm sorry to interrupt." She smiled at me. "I stood outside on the deck, but finally, I thought I had better come in before your very interested neighbor on the other side called the police."

"That's all right." I stretched out my hand to her, wondering if she was half as nervous as Cathryn was. "We were just discussing something, but it will keep." I inclined my head to the doorway. "Shall we?"

"Hail, hail, the gang's all here." Rafe stood up as I came into the living room. Lucas and Veronica were on my heels, and I couldn't help sneaking a peek at Cathryn's face. As always, she appeared to be perfectly aloof and serene, showing not even a wit of emotion.

"We are indeed, and we have beer." I offered bottles to Rafe and Nell, who both took them gladly, and then after a beat of hesitation, held out a bottle to Cathryn. I fully expected her to decline, as I'd never seen her drink anything less refined than a glass of red wine, but she accepted it and took a deep swig.

Nervous drinker, much? I thought and then winced when I saw her roll her eyes. I'd never get used to my thoughts not being private around her.

"Jackie, how's Mrs. Mac? I'm sorry we weren't down here for the pageant." Rafe patted my arm. "I heard that it was pretty eventful."

"Oh, you know . . . just attempted murder, near death and a new beauty queen crowned. All in a day's work."

"What happened exactly? Lucas said the murderer was a real estate agent."

I nodded. "He'd made a deal with a developer in the area who wanted the land where Golden Rays is located. If Augustus Row could convince a certain percentage of residents to list their homes, this developer was going to buy the houses and pay him a bonus. I guess Augustus had a gambling problem and needed the payout, so he was desperate enough to do anything he could to get that payment."

"So it wasn't connected to the pageant at all?" Nell shook her head. "Crazy."

"Apparently not. Row just took advantage of the opportunity of the pageant to try to kill Mrs. Mac. He was also hoping to use the publicity of offing pageant contestants to convince more people to sell their houses." I shrugged. "Not exactly a very well-thought out or considered plan, but that was his motive." I glanced up at Veronica, who stood staring at Cathryn. "Sorry. I didn't mean to get us off-topic." We all fell silent.

"Cathryn." Veronica stepped up next to her granddaughter's chair. "I'm glad to meet you face-to-face at last." She extended one pale slim hand.

For a few awkward seconds, I was afraid Cathryn was going to ignore her, but finally, she took the offered hand.

"What should I call you? Great Grandmother?"

The other woman laughed. "Veronica is fine. I shouldn't like to think of the odd looks we'd get if you called me Grammy out in public, when I don't look more than a few years older than you are."

In reality, of course, Veronica was physically younger than Cathryn. She'd only been about twenty when Diego had turned her. But she was giving her granddaughter a small offering, a gesture of good-will.

Cathryn nodded. "That was you in Cape May. That night."

"It was, and I'm sorry I didn't make myself known. I was still . . . researching. Learning." She took a seat on the sofa and smiled at the others. "Rafe and Nell. It's such a pleasure to meet you both. I'm Veronica Carruthers."

"Of course you are," Nell murmured, but she was smiling.

"I'm glad you're here, actually. It's nice to have someone more bizarre than me in our group."

Veronica laughed again. "I'll take that for the compliment it's meant to be. I'm honored to meet such a gifted witch." Her gaze shifted. "And Rafe . . . you scoundrel. I'm only glad that our paths didn't cross before now, or I'm sure I would've fallen prey to your charms."

Rafe cocked one eyebrow. "The good news is that I'm taken now, permanently. But yeah, if we'd met before, I can't imagine I wouldn't have gone after you."

"All right. Can we stop talking about how you would've hit on my grandmother?" Cathryn had an edge in her voice. "We have many things to discuss. Nell, would you please check the perimeter and cast the protections?"

The witch nodded, and her eyes slid shut. I sat perfectly still, watching as her hands lifted, her fingers twitching. Finally, she opened her eyes and nodded.

"We're good. Proceed as you like."

Cathryn nodded. "I have a good deal of information to share with you, and then we have plans to make. Let's start at the beginning." Her eyes flickered to Veronica. "Thanks to what Veronica has confirmed to us, we know more about the genesis of the demon coming into this world and how it has moved about since that time. We know that the ultimate plan involves a ritual in April, exactly fifty years after the first ceremony, at the time that is the actual prescribed date to bring the entire contingent of demons over into this world. We know that right after the door between worlds has been opened, the rest of their plan will go into action. It involves war, bloodshed and violence. It will spell the end of the world for everyone.

"Unless we can stop it."

Lucas reached for my hand and held it tight. None of this was new, per se, but hearing it stated in such stark, matter of fact terms was all the more chilling. Across the room, Nell blinked at me. She wasn't flipping out, but there was a glimmer of understanding and compassion in her eyes. I remembered two things then: one, Nell had dealt with this evil before. She'd fought them, and she'd come out the other side. It was true that what she and Rafe had fought was a somewhat lesser, weaker version, but still . . . they'd both survived. And two, Nell's mother was involved with this group. She'd tried to lure Nell into joining them, and it was only Nell's connection to Rafe and his love that had saved her.

"Do we have a plan?" Lucas spoke in an even tone. "And not to be flippant, Cathryn, but do we have a plan that's more solid than your 'let's bring Delia back from the Great Beyond' plan? Because if you didn't notice, that one had flaws."

"*Omnia causa fiunt.*" Veronica kept her eyes trained on Cathryn. "Everything happens for a reason. And in this case, the miscalculation is what brought Joss back, isn't it? As it turns out, I think having her is going to be a great help to our cause."

"Really?" I couldn't quite imagine how this was going to work. "Because last time I checked, Joss was tethered to her townhouse. And being non-corporeal and all, that makes her a little less than handy when it comes to fighting. Also, when we're talking about everything happening for a reason, I didn't so much enjoy the being possessed part. I'd like to skip that next time, if no one minds."

"If Joss hadn't come over as she had, and if Delia hadn't possessed you, we wouldn't have the information that we do," Veronica reminded me. "Delia wouldn't have spoken to anyone else except Joss. I understand that it was a difficult time, but everyone came out on the other side. Now we move on."

Across the room, Rafe caught my eye and winked at me. He and I had had long discussions about what had happened to me, and his advice had gone a long way to helping me deal with the aftermath of possession. I knew he understood how I felt better than anyone else in the room.

"Joss is important and necessary, and we are putting pieces in place that will allow her to move." Cathryn finished her beer, set the bottle on the floor at her feet, and folded her hands in her lap. "We won't be safe at the townhouse or even at the Carruthers headquarters in the long run. We're working on other options. Better ones. But meanwhile, I need you all to prepare. Jackie, Lucas tells me you've begun setting up your business to run in your absence. That's excellent. Rafe has spoken to his grandparents, and we're attempting to make arrangements for their safety."

"What about my family?" I leaned toward Cathryn. "What about my parents, my brothers and their wives and kids, and my friends here? Are you making 'arrangements' for them, too?" I knew that Rafe's grandparents were wealthy bigwigs in their community. They both had extraordinary gifts, as well. But I didn't see how that made them any more important than my loved ones.

"Of course we have." Cathryn's words were clipped. "There will be agents both here and up in New York who will be guarding your family, and in the event that they were threatened, they would be moved to a safe house. But we're trying to allow everything to go along as normal for as long as possible. That's in everyone's best interest."

I nodded. I understood her point, and her rationale was solid, but I'd needed to hear it from her own lips. I'd needed her word that the important people in my life weren't going to be abandoned if she could help it.

"The plan that we're evolving . . . it's complicated, and it's going to take time to put into place. Additionally, we're going to need to recruit people. Carruthers has a large roster of people with amazing, unique talents, but over the years, we've focused on those who can use their gifts to help others in some way. That means that we're somewhat limited. We've discovered that there are others out there in the world whom we never dreamed existed. We need some of them to help us. So for the next few months, I'll be traveling in order to secure commitments from these people."

"What are we talking here, Cathryn?" Lucas cocked his head. "Werewolves? Zombies? We've already got a witch and two vampires right here."

"I'm not going to dignify that question with an answer," she shot back. "Whoever elects to join us will gather at the appointed time and place. I hope I can talk all of them into fighting with us, but I'm not naïve. I know there are some who will prefer to sit out the fight and see who wins before they choose sides. And I also know some will elect to go with the dark side. There's an element among the gifted who resent ordinary humans for whatever lack of acceptance or prejudice they've experienced in their lives. Those will be intrigued with the idea of a world where the extraordinary have an upper hand, and they won't listen to reason. They'll allow their own narrow focus and viewpoints to blind them to the greater good." She sounded sad, and I felt bad for giving her a hard time earlier.

It was easy to forget sometimes how hard Cathryn worked and how completely she had dedicated her life thus far to her family's cause. She was often stiff and cool; she rarely showed emotion. But she was passionate about this fight, and I knew she would sacrifice everything to make sure we were ready when the time came.

"When and where will we gather?" This time, the question came from Veronica. "And . . . will I be permitted to be part of the planning and the fight? I promise, I'm useful in a battle. I want to help. This is important to me."

Cathryn's hesitation was barely perceptible. "Of course. We need every hand on deck. As to the when and where, that will be sent to you at the right time. In order to preserve the safe parameters, we won't disclose the location until the very last moment. We don't want the Hive to attack us before we're assembled and ready."

"Do you really expect an attack?" Nell sounded surprised. "I'd think they'd be so focused on their own plans that they'd mostly ignore us. We've been laying low for a while. We haven't done much to threaten them."

"They haven't been ignoring us, and you know that." Cathryn sighed. "All the little fires you and Rafe have been working to put out over the last few months have been their attempts at distraction. When they realize that we're serious, that we're organizing to challenge them, I expect their human leadership to do anything they can to derail our plans."

"I agree." Rafe nodded. "So you're going on a recruiting trip, Cathryn. Are you bringing in any other existing agents to supplement the team, or will they be guarding the home front?"

"Most of our current agents will not be privy to our

plans or our location. After what happened with both Emma and Delia, I'm very concerned about the existence of other double agents. Not even the leadership at Harper Creek will know where we are, once we're in place." She paused, and her eyes met Rafe's. "But since I've been accused before of hiding things that might upset some of you, I should probably tell you this. After I leave here today, I'll be making a trip down to King. I'm going to try to convince Tasmyn Vaughn—well, she's Tasmyn Sawyer now—to join us."

I held my breath. I didn't know Tasmyn, but I knew of her. After Veronica had mentioned her name to us, I'd asked Nell to give me the full scoop on the girl. I understood that her powers were not unlike Nell's and Cathryn's; she could hear thoughts, and she could also move objects and practice elemental magic. Unlike Nell and Cathryn, however, Tasmyn had been raised to hide her abilities. It had only been when her family moved to King, Florida, that she began to develop those gifts.

Of course, it was also in King that Nell had tried to kill Tas while they were still in high school, and where Tasmyn had met Rafe when he moved to town during their senior year. I knew from conversations with Nell that Rafe had fancied himself in love with Tas, and when she'd chosen her boyfriend Michael over him, that heartbreak had launched Rafe on his summer of man-whoring, as he called it.

I was a little murky on the details, but I'd heard that Nell had redeemed herself by astral projecting back to King from the mental hospital where she'd been committed and helping to save Tasmyn from the crazed witch-teacher who was attempting to kidnap her. The blood ritual that had allowed her to project had also caused her to fall into a deep coma, until

Cathryn and some others from Carruthers had worked their mojo to wake her up so that she could save Rafe's life.

I thought Nell had made her peace with Tasmyn, but still . . . I wondered how she'd feel about working side-by-side with the woman who was not only her former victim but also her boyfriend's past love. Of course, I myself had some experience with that, as here in this room were not only one but two of my boyfriend's ex-lovers. *And* they were from the same family. How messed up was that?

Both Cathryn and Veronica swiveled their heads to look at me, nearly identical expressions on their similar faces, reminding me that when two mind-hearers were in the vicinity, my thoughts were not my own. I gave a little shrug. They'd just have to deal with it.

"I think *not* asking Tasmyn to help us would be a huge mistake." Nell crossed her legs. "She's powerful, and she has that inerrant sense of right and wrong, doesn't she? Plus, she went up against Ben Ryan. I think she'll be compelled to want to see this through."

Rafe didn't speak right away, but finally, he nodded. "Nell's right. Tasmyn's too strong to leave her on the sidelines. Now, the bigger question will be whether or not she wants in. Last thing I heard was that she was working hard *not* to use her powers. She left Carruthers after only a few months, and she seems to be focusing on having a normal life." He slid a glance sideways to Nell. "So she's married now, is she?"

Nell shifted. "Apparently so. I'm happy for her. She and Michael deserve to find their happy ending."

Rafe muttered something under his breath, but Nell pretended not to hear.

"Excellent." Cathryn looked a little relieved. I wondered if she'd been that worried about how Nell and Rafe might react to bringing Tasmyn into our team. "While I'm in King, Rafe, I'm going to stop in to see your grandparents. Ostensibly, I'll be there to find out if there's anyone else I should consider inviting to join us, but I'll also try to talk them into going underground for a time."

"Thank you." Rafe's mouth twisted into a half-smile. "It won't work. They're both stubborn cusses, and they think we might need them once things get serious, but it means something that you'll try. I appreciate it."

"Where will you go after King?" Veronica touched her granddaughter's arm. "Is there anything I can do? I'd be happy to travel with you. I still have connections here and there."

Cathryn looked grim. "Thanks. After King, I'll be heading for Ireland. If my mission there succeeds, I'll feel much better about our chances of winning this battle." She regarded Veronica for a moment. "How do you feel about a trip to Louisiana? There's a woman named Sionnach Creven I'd like on our side. I've traced her as far as New Orleans. She's a tough nut, but you could give it a shot, if you wanted."

Rafe perked up. "I wouldn't mind a trip to New Orleans." He smirked. "I have some very happy memories of that city."

"No, Rafe." Nell's voice was mild and amused, but her face was adamant. "We have our own mission."

He gave an exaggerated sigh. "Everyone else gets to have fun but us."

"If we live through this, I promise you a month-long stay in New Orleans, just the two of us. How does that sound?" Nell twined her fingers with Rafe's.

"Sounds like heaven." He smiled, and my heart melted a little. On paper, Rafe and Nell shouldn't have worked, but damn . . . there was no denying their chemistry.

"All right then." Cathryn stood up, gazing at each of us in turn. "Everyone has orders. Stay alert, stay alive and be ready to move on a moment's notice."

"Will you tell me more about this Sionnach I'm to find?" Veronica stood, too, her eyes tentative as she watched Cathryn.

"Yes, I can give you the rundown on her." She ran the tip of her tongue across her lips. "Why don't you ride up to Harper Creek with me? I know my mother wants to meet you, and I can fill you in on everything as we drive. You're welcome to stay with us as long as you like."

Veronica smiled, and it was like the sun rising over the placid sea. I knew she was treading carefully, aware that she couldn't push Cathryn too far too fast, but her eagerness to interact with her family was so apparent. I was glad that she would have this chance.

The two Carruthers women left us, and Rafe and Nell followed them out the door. Rafe wrapped me in a tight hug.

"Try not to worry, Jacks, okay?" He pressed his lips to the top of my head in a brotherly kiss. "It's all going to be all right. In a few months, we'll be kicking back with champagne, celebrating the fact that this messed-up world is still spinning. And we'll look back on this time and laugh."

I closed my eyes and leaned against him. "Promise?"

"You know it, baby." He released me. "Nell and I need to hit the road. But we'll be in touch. Call if anything pops up, okay? And give Mrs. Mac and Charlie our love. Tell them we'll see them . . . next time."

Rafe was trying to be light and teasing, but in his eyes, I saw the truth. There wouldn't be any more improptu, impulsive visits down to see us. No more double dates, at least for the time being; no more playing around.

Our fun was over. It was time to concentrate on saving the world.

The End

Epilogue

"ARE YOU AWAKE?"

I didn't answer Jackie right away. We'd both been a little quiet since Rafe, Nell, Cathryn and Veronica had left, both of us keeping our own counsel as we went about the rest of the day. By tacit agreement, we'd both gone to bed at her house, and she'd kissed me goodnight before we turned off the lights. But even though empathy and mind hearing weren't my gifts, I could practically feel her worry.

Rolling over, I pulled her close so that her ear pressed into my chest. "Yeah, I'm awake. I thought you'd dropped off hours ago, though."

"No." Her voice was muffled against me. "Lucas . . . aren't you even the slightest bit frightened?"

I tightened my arms around her. "Of course I am. I'm fucking terrified. Any person in his right mind would be right now. We're facing a fight that could mean the end of the world."

"I looked around that room today, and I thought . . . there are six of us here. The odds aren't good that all of us will survive to celebrate afterwards."

"Isn't it Han Solo who says, 'Never tell me the odds.'?" Quoting *Star Wars* was always a good way to change the subject.

She sighed. "Don't try to distract me or tease. I'm serious."

I nodded, though I knew she couldn't see me. "I am, too. I know you're right. But worrying about it isn't giong to help us. The best thing we can do is to be prepared. And we're doing everything we can."

"Hmmm." Her voice vibrated against my skin, making me shiver. "Why didn't you tell me that you'd increased how much blood you're drinking?"

I'd known this was coming, too. "I don't know. I could claim that it was because we were distracted with the murders and worrying over Mrs. Mac, but that wouldn't be completely true. I guess I knew it would upset you, and . . . I didn't want you to think I was drinking more from the bags instead of from you."

She was silent. I trailed my fingers down the column of her spine, feeling each familiar bump. I wasn't sure sometimes that Jackie realized how precious she was to me. Our lives had been a rollercoaster of insanity since we'd met, with me coming to grips over who and what I was, the various murders we'd encountered, and now the impending doom breathing down our necks. But I wished I could prove to her that none of that mattered when it was just the two of us, together.

"I didn't think that," she answered me at last. "And when I consider it rationally, it does make sense that you're gearing up for this fight. What Veronica told us was that she turned you specifically to give our side an advantage in the battle. She said that you being a half-vamp increases your effectiveness as a death broker and makes you a better fighter overall. So maybe you need to drink extra blood to feed that power."

"Maybe." I let my hand wander down to her firm, round ass. "I try not to talk too much about drinking blood because I know it bothers you. I think sometimes you can pretend I'm just a normal guy with an unusual job, except for the blood. That's the part of me that freaks you out."

"You're probably right. I'm sorry." She tilted her head up so that I could see her eyes. Even in the dark, I could feel their warmth. "It's not that I don't understand or accept the vampire part of you. But that part does feel a little . . . wilder. A little less controllable."

"There's nothing to be sorry for. But never forget . . . the blood is something I need, but you're my real source of strength. You're what keeps me going. You're my reason for wanting to fight to keep this world turning."

She was staring up at me still. "Remember the first night I kissed you? You told me then that my blood made you crazy. You said you craved me, and you'd never craved anyone else to that point."

I smiled. "It was the truth. It's still the truth."

"You still want me? My blood is still the only one you want to drink?" There was doubt in her voice, and I understood. Meeting Veronica had made Jackie second-guess her own role in my life. But even though Veronica had turned me, Jackie would forever be the one woman I chose above all others.

"Always." I nudged her lips up to me and covered them

with mine. "You give me everything I need, baby. You fill up spots in me that I didn't even know were there until I met you. I want your body, I want your blood . . . but I also want your heart and your soul. I want to consume all of you, and I want to give myself to you."

"I want to give you everything I have." She rolled over until she lay on top of me, the heat between her legs cradling my throbbing cock.

Framing her face with both of my hands, I threaded my fingers through her hair. "When we're together, whether we're alone or with others, I can hear your heartbeat. I've heard it since the first day we met. No one else's. Only yours. And each beat is the most beautiful music in the world to me."

"Each beat belongs to you and only you." She surged up, kissing me with a new intensity before she rose onto her knees and sank down onto me, taking me inside her and driving me crazy with pleasure as she rocked.

I groaned. "I love you, baby. I only want you. Ride me hard."

Jackie bowed her body forward, offering me her breast and holding my neck as I arched to take the rosy nipple into my mouth.

"Drink. Drink from me. I want you . . . I want to be inside you, just like you're inside me."

A frenzied blindness swept over me at her words, and without asking another question, I sank my teeth into her soft flesh and drank deep, taking in her strength the only way I knew, as I pumped into her and we both cried out in our fevered climax.

And when she fell onto me, boneless and spent, our hearts beat in synchronicity.

The story continues . . .

Follow Cathryn to Ireland in
Moonlight on the Meadow
January 24, 2017

And meet Sionnach in Hotel Paranormal's
The Fox's Wager
February 1, 2017.

And of course . . .
See how the batle ends in
Age of Aquarius
April 7, 2017.

If you enjoyed this book, please tell a friend!

The best way to do this is to leave a review on your favorite ebook vendor's site, or post on social media (tag me!) or recommend my books to your friends.

And please do chat with me on Facebook, Instagram or Twitter, visit my website and join the Naughty Temptresses.

Thank you!

Acknowledgements

If it's October 31st, it must be time for another Death book!

This part of Jackie and Lucas's story has been playing in my mind since I finished writing Death A La Mode last year. Even though I took a year off from releasing paranormal, I've continued to work on all of the upcoming books, so they were never far from my thoughts. I know there are a lot of open ends, but I promise, we'll see tons of resolution between now and April 7th. Be sure that you've read ALL the paranormal books so you're ready!

Thank you first and foremost to my awesome beta readers, Kara Schilling, Krissy Smith, Carla Edmonson and Marla Wenger. You all rock on short notice and with very few days. Hearts and kisses all around.

Meg Murrey designed this awesome cover, and I love it! Thank you so much. Stacey Blake from Champagne Formats made it all so pretty on the inside~wine and hugs to YOU!

I was on a looming deadline for this book while Mandie Stevens and I were making Indie BookFest 2016 happen (in the middle of Hurricane Matthew). I finished it the week after IBF16, and some of the names in the book owe a debt to our venue this year. Thank you to Mandie for being my business partner and best friend! Next year? More wine, more giggles and more relaxation. Right?

My dear Olivia Hardin gave me the idea of the Ms. Florida Senior Living Pageant—thank you! Love you, my under-the-rock partner.

Thanks to Heather Hildenbrand and Jill Cooper, my sprinting partners, who kept me hitting word count goals. Big hugs to both you lovely ladies.

As always, love to my Temptresses for their cheering, their support and their listening ears. And to my family . . . thanks for your patience, your understanding and your love. Love you all big time!

Playlist

I Will Follow You Into the Dark—Death Cab for Cutie

Vampires Will Never Hurt You—My Chemical Romance

We're in This Together—Nine Inch Nails

Let Love Bleed Red—Sleeping with Sirens

Clocks—Coldplay

I Belong to You—Muse

Special Extra Scenes!

I've been privileged to be a Featured Author at Coastal Magic Convention for the past five years. For the last few Halloweens, the owner and organizer, Jennifer Morris, has hosted as many of us who like on her website, offering a flash fic opportunity. We're given a file of pictures from which to choose, and then we write a short piece inspired by that art.

Last year and this year, my flash fiction involved characters from Recipe for Death and the Serendipity books. I'm going to share them both with you as bonus content here, although at least one will probably make it into AGE OF AQUARIUS in one form or another.

Enjoy!

SCENE ONE (Thanks to Mandie Stevens for lending me both characters and setting for this one!)

"That was one of the best dinners I've ever eaten that I didn't cook." I dabbed my mouth with the linen napkin and sat back in my chair. "But now I don't think I can move."

Lucas smiled as he sipped his wine. "Good news is that you don't have to move far. Aren't you glad now that we decided to get a hotel room for tonight?"

"Yeah, yeah, whatever. You were right. I just hope Makani's not giving Mrs. Mac any trouble. Normally I wouldn't worry, but with tonight being Halloween, he's going to be crazy." My dog was normally pretty chill, but dozens of trick or treaters set him on edge.

"I warned her about letting him get hopped on sugar. I think he'll be safe." He reached for my hand then jerked upright, away from me. "Shit. *Shit.* Jackie, I'm sorry, but I'm being summoned to a Reckoning. I need to get someplace private to transport."

I sat up, too, and pointed to the back of the courtyard where we were eating. "There's the alley we cut through on our way here. Now that it's dark, you'll probably be safe there."

"Okay." He stood up, pushing back his chair, and leaned down to kiss my lips quickly. "I'll get back as fast as I can. Are you all right to walk to the hotel by yourself? If you feel uncomfortable, call a taxi."

"I will, but don't worry about me. I'll be fine." I lowered my voice. "When your boyfriend's a vampire slash death broker, you don't spook easily."

Lucas rolled his eyes, but he didn't have time for anything else. As he jogged away, our waitress approached the table.

"Everything okay?" She frowned at the back of my departing date, probably thinking I'd been ditched.

"Yep!" I gave her a bright smile. "My boyfriend . . . uh, his job sometimes calls him away."

She nodded. "He's a doctor?"

"Something like that."

I paid the bill and left, wandering down the narrow side streets of St. Augustine. I'd been here before often enough that I knew my way around this part of town, the old city across from the Fort. The shops and cobblestone streets were familiar, though tonight they seemed just a little spookier, a little more mysterious than they usually did.

After all, it was Halloween.

I knew I should go back to the hotel and wait for Lucas. Reckonings, where he was required to determine the final destination of just-departed souls, could move quickly or take hours, depending on how much of a fight the advocates for light and dark put up. But the idea of sitting in the room by myself, channel surfing, sounded too pathetic. I decided it wouldn't hurt to wander a bit.

The streets and alleys were crowded, with more people wearing costumes than not. Sometimes it was hard to tell which ones were children and which were adults. I paused outside the spice store, watching the parade of witches, ghouls, monsters and vampires pass, amusing myself by picking out which ones really existed—to my knowledge—and which ones did not.

Jackie.

I startled, glancing around, but the voice seemed to drift by me, as though it had floated in on the sea breeze.

Jaaaaackie. . .

A shiver of dread gave me goose bumps. I was about to push off the wall and head back toward the hotel when I felt a hand on my shoulder. I froze as a strong sense of déjà vu swept over me. Not long ago, I'd had an encounter with Veronica, the mysterious woman who'd apparently changed Lucas into a vampire. I hadn't known who she was at the time, but ever since, I'd been a little jumpy, seeing creepy vampires around every corner.

Wheeling around, I relaxed when I saw a tall blonde woman I didn't recognize. *Not Veronica.* She stepped back when she saw my face.

"Oh, I'm sorry. I thought—I was meeting someone here, and I thought you were her." Her eyes narrowed.

"Are you all right? You look like you've seen a ghost."

"At least a dozen of them." I pointed behind me at the costumed people, grinning. When the woman only tilted her head, frowning, I shrugged. "You startled me a little. I thought *you* were someone else, too."

"You look as though you could use a drink." She hesitated, as though debating something as she glanced over my shoulder. "Come on. I know a place where—well, just come on."

She grabbed hold of my hand and hauled me down the road a little. Apprehension prickled at the back of my neck as the woman kept looking behind us, as though she saw something I couldn't.

"I'm Jackie, by the way." I trotted to keep her from pulling off my arm. "And um, my boyfriend is expecting me back at our hotel. I really should—"

"I'm Eva. And he's not back yet." She scowled. "Damn it. Here." She pulled me around the corner, and suddenly we were on damp stone steps that led up a narrow passage between two imposing walls. The moon shone through the wispy clouds, illuminating Eva's face. She had an almost other-worldly sense about her, an elusive something I'd seen in our friends Nell and Rafe. And when I'd mentioned Lucas, she'd replied, *He's not back yet.*

"Who are you?" I meant the words to sound like a demand, but they came out as a whisper.

She flicked a glance at me. "I'm a friend. And you were being followed. Don't worry. I won't let anyone hurt you. I know where we can go to be safe." She shot me a half-smile. "But you're going to have to trust me."

Without waiting for a response, Eva took off up the steps, and I had no choice but to follow her. The passage turned to become a long hallway bathed in pitch-black darkness. I kept moving, groping along the wall until I heard a creak and dim light shone through a rough-hewn wooden door.

Eva slipped through the opening, standing back to let me in before she closed the door behind us. I heard muffled noise below us.

"Where are we?"

"Nowhere you've ever been." She beckoned me forward. "We'll be okay if we get downstairs. I think, anyway."

We crept down a winding iron stair case, and the hum of voices and laughter swelled. At the bottom of the steps, Eva paused and glanced back at me.

"We're going into a bar now. It's called Spellbound, and you're going to see some, uh, interesting types here. Don't talk to anyone unless I say, don't make eye contact, and stick close to me."

"I thought you said it was safe." I wasn't feeling particularly reassured.

"It is, relatively speaking." Her lips quirked into a sardonic smile. "You're going to learn, probably sooner than later, that there's no place truly safe."

When Eva had said I'd see some interesting types, I'd pictured a typical bar scene. And in some ways, I wasn't wrong. But as we darted between groups and wound our way to the bar itself, I began to suspect some of these people weren't dressed in costumes. They looked eerily real. And some of them stared just a little too long as Eva and I pushed past.

"No eye contact," she muttered just before she pushed me forward to the bar. I caught myself with both hands and glared at her.

"Eva, what the hell?" The man behind the counter was huge, and instantly I thought, *Viking*. He crossed his massive arms over his chest and stared down at us.

"Soren, not now. I was looking for—well, it doesn't matter at the moment. I was supposed to meet someone, but then there were demons after this one." She pointed at me. "I didn't have anywhere else to bring her."

He raised one eyebrow. "So you brought her . . . here?"

She scowled. "It's Halloween. There're all kinds of humans in here."

"Fine, but what're you going to do with her after midnight? And don't even think about throwing down with any demon types in my place. Not tonight. Any of them followed you in here and go after her, I'm kicking all your asses out the door." He let his eyes fall almost shut. "Unless you want to make it worth my while *not* to do that."

Eva growled under her breath, and I could hear the frustration. I licked my lips and stood taller, beginning to creep away.

"Listen, why don't I solve everybody's problems by going back to my hotel? My boyfriend's probably freaking out waiting for me."

Both of the blondes turned as though they'd forgotten about me until I spoke. Eva started to reply, but Soren interrupted her.

"I have a better idea. Why don't you just come back to my office? I can protect you . . . in privacy." He smiled at me, and the light glinted off dangerous white teeth. A chill ran down my back.

Eva sucked in a breath, but before she could say anything else, a hand closed around my arm. "Jackie. Thank God." Lucas folded me into his body, and I sagged against him in relief.

"How did you know where to find me?" My words were muffled against his chest.

He sighed. "It's a long story, but basically, this was a setup. I could tell from the beginning something was wonky with the Reckoning. The advocate for the dark kept hemming and hawing, long after I knew what the outcome would be. Finally, the advocate for light accused him of stalling, and we managed to find out what was going on." He looked grim. "The light advocate told me where you would be."

"Eva saved me." I glanced at her over my shoulder.

Lucas's arms tightened around me. "Thank you."

She shrugged. "Right place, right time." Her lips pressed together. "But I need to go. There's someone else I'm supposed to be with right now. You got this?"

"We're good." Lucas nodded.

Eva started to leave and then stopped, looking back. "It's coming. It's getting closer. You're right the hell in the middle of this, and there are forces that would do anything to stop you. You need to know that. There's no such thing as safe anymore."

With that, she turned and disappeared into the crowd. Lucas watched her go and then took my hand.

"Let's get out of here."

We threaded our way through the crowd and out into the uncertain darkness.

Scene Two: (Takes place after DEATH OVER EASY)

Dried leaves skittered across the stone steps of the mausoleum. The sky was cloudy tonight, but as Nell and I approached the edge of the cemetery, there was just enough moonlight to read the name chiseled over the two heavy doors with their brass pulls. Dead vines teased the top of the word, but I could see enough to make it out.

Next to me, Nell shivered. It was much cooler up here than what we were used to in Florida. I draped one arm around her shoulders and drew her closer to my side.

"Hover." She murmured the name, squinting in the darkness. "That's the one, then?"

I nodded. "I think so. I don't see any other bone mansions around here with that name."

"We're a long way from San Francisco." Her pale blue eyes roamed over the overgrown grass of the old burial yard. "How did the talisman end up in Virginia?"

"After those five men tried to open the dimensional door for the aliens—who turned out to be demons—they all had mental breaks. Our guy was brought back here to his hometown. As far as we know, they put the necklace in his coffin when he died."

"Lovely." Nell shrugged. "Well, let's get started. The sooner we get this, the sooner we can get out of here." She glanced over her shoulder. "There's . . . unrest here."

"No shit," I muttered under my breath. Nell didn't pay attention to me; she'd already closed her eyes and lifted her hands. I knew the hands were more for her own focus than anything else, as all the power came from her mind.

At first, nothing happened beyond the wind picking up a

little. And then there was a low groaning, and ever so slowly, the huge doors began to scrape and creak open. As soon as they did, the odor of decay poured out, making me gag.

Nell wasn't affected at all. She dropped her hands back to her sides and climbed the steps, leaving me to follow behind her.

"Rafe, do you have your flashlight? I don't think it's likely that there'll be electric lighting in here."

"Got it." I clicked on the button and pointed the light into the pitch black of the burial chamber. Shelves lined both sides, and caskets had been slid onto each one. I hesitated, not sure which would be the most likely to be the one we needed, but Nell moved unerringly to the top coffin on the right.

"This one? You sure?"

She cast me a wry look. "We've got to start somewhere, and I think it's most likely to be one of the more recent ones, which means a top shelf. If you let me climb on your shoulders, I should be able to open it up and see inside."

I obliged, kneeling so that she could toss one jean-covered leg over my neck. Rising, I grasped her thighs, eliciting a soft hiss from Nell when my fingers strayed too far off course. Well, who could blame a guy for taking advantage of his hot girlfriend in this position?

"Almost got it open." She sounded strained and breathless, and I was just opening my mouth to tease her about that when a small noise behind us made me freeze. An icy-cold hand closed around my arm, and a low voice growled near my ear, sending a chill of dread down my spine.

"What the hell do you think you're doing with my coffin?"

Printed in the USA
CPSIA information can be obtained
at www.ICGtesting.com
JSHW031714140824
68134JS00038B/3686